Best Friends

by Hope Benton
Illustrator Lynne Srba

Open Minds, Inc., TM *Columbus, Ohio, 1996*

i

The Best Friends series provide an alternative to children's
literature with fictional stories based on real life stories of
inclusion. Open Minds,™ Inc. through literature hopes to affect
"real inclusion" through the subtle focus on the challenges that
differently able children face.

Open Minds,™ Inc. and the author provide this disclaimer to those
who read the Best Friend stories. The author's and publisher's
intent in minimizing the focus on the challenges is in no way an
attempt to minimize the effect of actual challenges that the full
spectrum of differently able children or adults face.   Rather, the
author has chosen to focus on the similarities among all children
regardless of abilities in order to provide a positive model for all
children. In so doing, it is the hope of the author and publisher that
"real inclusion" will occur as a result of able children reading these
stories.

Library of Congress Catalog Card Number: 96-92563

ISBN 1-888927-00-3 hardcover edition
ISBN 1-888927-78-X paperback edition

ii.

Open Minds,™ Inc.

A company that is dedicated to the creation of children's literature which celebrates the richness of differences, promotes attitudes of understanding and compassion, and models the inclusion of all individuals of society.

Inclusion is a challenge for the teachers, the parents, and most importantly the students. Focusing on the similarities among children rather than their differences provides a subtle but effective foundation for inclusion of all children regardless of their particular challenge in life.

As a result of reading literature which models subtle inclusion, children will come to conclusions on their own and will embrace inclusion. They will internalize healthy attitudes towards others with differences.

The Best Friends and Brothers Series are fictional stories based on the real life adventures and social relationships that the main characters have experienced.

Special Acknowledgments and Remembrances

My most sincere acknowledgment must go to my loving daughters, Kathryn and Sarah, and my husband Peter without whom there would be no reason to write. I love you!

Special acknowledgment must be given to my sisters Pamela Rigsbee, Barbara Beck, Linda Benton, Maura Benton, and to my brothers Clyde Benton and Donnie Benton, Jr. (deceased) who have been there for me throughout the years. They have been and continue to be a main source of strength.

Special acknowledgment and thanks to these dedicated volunteer readers, critics, and editors: John Beck, Barbara Beck, Katherine Beck, Maura Benton, Margaret Cloern, Nancy Kormanik and Pamela Rigsbee.

Acknowlegment and thanks must be given to Halle Ricker for being a special friend to Kathryn at this point in her life.

Special thanks to: Gretchen Ames, Helen Borghi, Margaret Cloern, Nancy Henceroth-Gatto, Suzanne Irwin, Nancy Kormanik, Carol Myers, and Nannette Scandaliato. Their belief in my ability to retell the story in a fictionalized version never wavered.

Special thanks and acknowledgment to "The Bagel Group" in Columbus, Ohio, for their friendship over the past years. They have helped me to move to the next stage of life with a new awareness of self and others.

Special acknowledgment must be given to those exemplary teachers and administrators in the Upper Arlington Public Schools and Columbus Public Schools in Ohio, who were able to open their minds and their hearts to embrace all children. Special thanks to the following administrators for meeting the challenge of inclusion before it was mandated: Shirley Wall, Homer Mincy, Phoebe Wienke, and Ted Oakley. And to the following educators who met the challenge in their own unique way: Heidi Gordon, Suzanne McConnell, Kim Diehr, Pat Owens, Donna Christman (Colerain), Gail Hall (Colerain), Laura Martin-Manser (Colerain), Charles Cozad (Colerain), Dawn Wendorf, Maureen Owens, Mr. Kowalik, Nancy Kaufmann, Debbie Sharp, Betsy O'Brochta, and others. Their model behavior and inclusive teaching have affected everyone. Without them, it would not be happening--there would be no inclusion stories to fictionalize.

Thanks to Mrs. Bonnie Emery and Mrs. Sherry Goubeaux, teachers in Upper Arlington, Ohio, along with Mrs. Pat Harris, and other teachers in Linwood, New Jersey, as well as Nannette Scandaliato in Boca Raton, Florida, for reading the earliest drafts of the book.

Thank you to Greta Seidman from Nevada, Katherine Beck and Kristin Claus from New Jersey, and Jessica Knisley and Katherine Wirick from Ohio, for their time and effort reading and commenting on the earliest drafts of the book.

Also, thank you to Lynne Srba, our illustrator, for being so wonderful to work with, so gifted and skilled as an artist. Thanks to Lynne our book covers are very special.

Finally, in remembrance of my mother and father, both deceased, who are my exceptional role models. They showed me through their actions how to raise a challenged child and what "real inclusion" means. They possessed forward thinking and openness when educating and raising a child who is both hearing and visually impaired. They were able to accomplish in the 1950s and 1960s what we are still working to do in the 1990s.

Hope

Dedicated to Kathryn Sarah, and Peter

Table of Contents

x.

1

No Sounds of Laughter

Singing was heard throughout the house. I flinched upon hearing the shrill sound of her voice. The singer of course was my mother. Songs sung out of tune filled the house whenever she was happy; and any complaints about her voice were all too often ignored. It had been like this for days.

Summer was coming to an end. That was the reason for her singing. The end of summer always made her sing and me cry. I turned around to look at the calendar on the wall. Yes, school would begin in a few days.

My mother was not only out of tune but in my room trying to reorganize my closet and our clothes for school. Not a good day.

Sarah, my younger sister, was in her room, reading her last mystery book of the summer. Books were among her most prized possessions.

"Sarah," I called to her as I left the kitchen.

No response! I knew that she was still reading.

My brain was churning with thoughts of practical jokes that I could play on her as I made my way slowly down the hall. Quietly turning into her room, my mouth widened into a grin at the thought of catching her off guard. Maybe I could surprise her.

Carefully, I entered her room and made it to the edge of her bed without making a sound. She hadn't heard me or at least she hadn't moved. Without the slightest bit of warning, I flopped onto her perfectly arranged bed; everything went flying.

Sarah turned and looked at me with a glare in her eye and an angry expression on her face. Oh, if looks could kill, I would have been dead.

"Cut it out, Kathryn," Sarah yelled.

"Come on Sarah, stop reading! School starts soon enough," I pleaded.

"Please, get off of my bed and pick up my stuff," Sarah said. "I would like to finish reading my book if you don't mind."

Reluctantly, I got off her bed and began putting her things back where they belonged.

"Well, you won't be reading for long. *Mother* wants us to do some work," I informed her.

Suddenly, as if on cue, we heard our mother calling us, "Sarah! Kathryn!"

"Seeee, I told youuuu!" I said.

I didn't wait for Sarah. Watching her read her book wasn't *that* much fun. I left, heading down the hall toward my room.

Shaking my head, I thought to myself, "If it was a computer game, now that would be a different story!"

Once inside, my eyes opened wide as I gazed around my bedroom. There was no sign of my mother. Where had she gone? And how could she have left my room in this condition? It was in shambles. It looked like a tornado had swept through it.

My room was filled with clothes that used to be in closets or in trunks. They were on the floor and on the bed in large heaps. It no longer looked like my bedroom. It was even more cluttered than I had ever made it.

"No one else's mother does this," I said aloud, wanting her to hear me wherever she was. "No one!"

Then a smile appeared on my face as I thought about my friend, Linda. She would have had a thing or two to say about this disaster.

It didn't help matters that my bedroom was the closest to the attic. Mother always brought Sarah's clothes into my room and repeated her "cleansing of the closets" (as she referred to it) marking summer's end.

At that moment, mother returned looking tired and breathing heavy. Her long brown hair was half in and half out of her familiar ponytail and her arms were filled with large cardboard boxes for packing. She put down the boxes then took a deep breath exhaling slowly. "Where's your sister?" she asked in her deep voice, as she began sorting clothes.

"Sarah's coming. She has a few more pages of her book to read," I replied.

Saddened by the shortness of summer, I asked, "Mom, why does summer disappear so quickly? The school year seems to go on forever and ever."

"I don't know Kathryn, it just does," she replied with unusual gentleness. "Kathryn, please help me to finish by trying on the clothes. The sooner we do it, the sooner we'll be finished."

"Okay," I agreed.

"Good," she replied. "Please put the ones that don't fit on the chair."

As soon as she turned away, I rushed to hide under the nearest pile of clothes. Being short and skinny, I had little trouble finding a hiding place. I submerged myself in old shirts and pants, peering through the armhole of one of the shirts, waiting and watching for Sarah to enter.

Well, where was she? What could be taking her so long?

Still undetected, I checked one more time just to make sure that I was completely hidden under the clothes. Confident that I was out of sight, I breathed a sigh of relief.

I froze when mother yelled, "Sarah!"

Seconds later, I saw her standing in the doorway, she seemed to be totally surprised by the condition of my room.

I knew what was going through her mind. She was happy it wasn't her room. It would have been a calamity if her room had been chosen because Sarah really disliked having her things out of order.

I continued watching her from my secret hiding place trying not to move or make a sound.

"Mother, where is Kathryn? Why isn't she helping?" Sarah wanted to know.

Mother who thought I was in the room, innocently replied, "Kathryn's right over_____?"

Before they said another word, I shot out of the pile of clothes like a rocket, straight up in the air. "Yeow!"

Coming out of hiding at just the right moment allowed me to catch Sarah completely by surprise. She fell over backwards, right smack on her behind and the book she was carrying went flying through the air.

"Kathryn, what are you doing?" my mother asked.

"Motherrrr! I can't find my book!" Sarah whined.

"Don't be such a baby, Sarah!" I shouted, annoyed that she couldn't take a joke.

Mother was getting aggravated. "Kathryn help your sister find her book," she said sternly, which meant that I'd better help to find it right away.

"Okay, okay," I said.

Usually, Sarah was the prankster in the family,

that is, when she wasn't reading her books.

"There it is! There's your book. It's under the bed," I told her, pointing with both of my index fingers.

Sarah didn't budge, not an inch.

So I reached down, grabbed her book, and tossed it to her. Still upset, not even a "thank you" passed her lips.

"Where are the clothes that you want me to try on, Mother?" Sarah asked, so sweetly that I thought I would be sick.

No sounds of laughter filled my room that day.

I had been silently observing them when my mother began talking about school. Half listening, I heard only bits and pieces of what she said.

In a split second, the mood in the room changed sending a shiver down my spine when my mother began to say the unthinkable, "School will make you more...."

"Mother!" I shouted. "Please don't say that word!" I pleaded, waving my arms.

My mother stood there with her hands on her hips, irritated by my reaction but I didn't care.

Sarah didn't look up but continued working as if nothing had happened.

I could sense my mother's gaze on my back as she continued to stare without saying a word for what seemed like a very long time.

Finally, she went back to putting the clothes that didn't fit in the marked boxes. Eventually, the look of concern disappeared from her face and her forehead became less wrinkled.

Still it was worth a temper tantrum even at my age to get her to stop using that horrible word. I hated that word because my parents were always nagging me about it.

I turned away wanting to forget what she had almost said aloud.

2

Last Night of Summer

"You two had better be in bed!" Mother yelled again. "You have to get up early tomorrow." She didn't realize that I was in Sarah's bedroom.

I wanted to stay up as late as I could. "When we wake up, summer will be officially over," I explained solemnly. "If we are very quiet, we can stay up longer because Mother will think that we've already gone to bed."

Not one to disobey, Sarah informed me, "We can't stay up late, Kathryn. We'll be tired tomorrow on our first day of school."

"Sure we can. We stay up late on 'sleepovers' with our friends, don't we?" I asked, trying to reason with her.

"Kathryn, you can't stop summer from ending," Sarah scolded, shaking her head and rolling her eyes.

"I know, Sarah. But I can try, can't I?" I replied sadly, dreading the end of summer.

Stretched comfortably across Sarah's bed, I was too tired to move. To concentrate on memories of summer was even difficult. The last days seemed to have gone by unnoticed, except by the few of us who wanted vacation to go on forever.

Sarah's closet door creaked and squeaked as she opened and closed it again and again.

Sarah just couldn't make up her mind. She went in and out of her closet for the thousandth time, searching for just the right outfit.

What would she wear? Would it be the right color? Would it fit? Would she be able to decide by morning?

"You look good in everything, Sarah," I told her truthfully.

"Thanks, Kathryn," Sarah replied only half listening.

Sarah couldn't make up her mind. But I knew that whatever she chose would be just right. She always found the perfect outfit! Or was it because everything looked perfect on Sarah?

"Sarah, don't you think that everyone always seems different after the summer vacation?" I asked.

"I guess so," Sarah mumbled. She was still busy looking over her wardrobe.

I sat quietly thinking about how some kids were always taller after the summer. Was it the summer weather that made everyone grow? Others looked more grown-up. Some came back with new haircuts or pierced ears. Yet some seemed unchanged.

Even though I should have guessed what her response would be, I decided to ask anyway, "Sarah, take a good look at me. Do you think that I have changed much this summer? Do I look more grown-up?"

"Of course you don't look different. You look the same to me. You just look like Kathryn!" Sarah replied with an air of certainty.

"Sarah, look again!" I said, trying to be serious. I sat up as tall as I possibly could; there was no stretch left in my body. "I know that I'm two inches taller for sure. It makes me look different, don't you think? Older?"

"And what about my hair?" I asked. "Should I cut it shorter? Would I be prettier if I did?"

I continued to stare at myself in the mirror near her bed. As I turned from the mirror to observe Sarah's reaction to my questions, I realized that she hadn't even been listening to me.

"Sarah! You haven't heard a word that I've said, have you?" I scolded her.

"What? What did you say Kathryn?" she asked.

"Oh, never mind," I replied, not wanting to repeat myself.

Suddenly, Sarah stopped what she was doing, walked over to me and looked me over from head to toe. She stood there staring at me, with her hand cupping her chin, pretending to be deep in thought.

"Well, you look the same to me, Kathryn!" she announced, covering her mouth with both hands, trying to stop from laughing.

"Sarah!" I shouted half-angry, half-fooling. I tried to grab her by the arm before she could get away. As usual, she got away just in time.

Hmmm...she had been listening to me all the time after all!

At that moment, we heard mother calling again, "Girls, get to bed now! And, I mean now!"

"Funny, Sarah! You're really funny!" I said, starting to leave her room. I needed to get to my room and into bed before Mother came to check on us.

With a silly smirk on her face, Sarah said, "I can't help it if you just look like Kathryn to me." She stood watching me as I rushed to get out of her room before Mother found me still up and about.

Making my way quickly down the hall, I breathed a sigh of relief once safely inside my own bedroom. There in the quiet of my room, I heard Sarah shout good night.

I pulled the covers over me and adjusted my pillow. Fighting sleep was useless; my eyelids were too heavy to keep open much longer. Laying in bed, I thought about what Sarah had said, wondering whether it was true--did I really just look like the same old Kathryn?

My dreams seemed to pass by at rapid speed, one after the other, all night long. I looked the same in every dream. Maybe I should have cut my hair shorter or pierced my ears.

My eyes seemed to be closed for only minutes as night slipped away, only to be replaced by the dawn. The singing of the birds could be heard through my bedroom window.

I lay in bed still sleepy-eyed, groggy and unable to move. Thoughts filled my head about the first day of school and all that it would bring. Then without any warning, a window shade flew open and sunlight burst into the room.

Looking through blurred vision and temporarily blinded by the bright sunlight, I was startled by the shadowy figure standing near the windows. Who was it? Straining to focus my eyes, I tried to identify the intruder. Even though it wasn't too difficult to guess who it was!

A second and then a third window shade flew open. "Motherrr!" I protested, knowing it was her all along.

Bending over me and touching my arm, she said, "Kathryn, today's the first day of school. It's time to get up."

"Just five more minutes! Please!" I begged.

"Kathryn, you need to get up now," she insisted, ignoring my request for more time.

Still in bed, my hand searched the nightstand for my eyeglasses. But I couldn't find them. I thought for sure that I had placed them there before going to sleep.

My arm stretched as my hand hunted under my bed for them.

The next thing I knew, my mother was handing them to me. "Thanks," I mumbled, putting them on right away so that I could see.

Before leaving my room, she informed me that I would miss the bus if I didn't get up and get dressed right away.

"Okay! Okay!" I replied. "I'm getting up." But I didn't. Instead, I lay in bed, with my eyeglasses on and my eyes closed, half awake and half asleep.

I had showered the night before which, lucky for me, meant a few more minutes of shut eye.

Off she went toward Sarah's room. I could hear the window shades flying up, as she woke Sarah. The cries of protest coming from her room made me smile. But Sarah was a morning person, so she would be up and about in no time.

"Kathryn, you won't have time for breakfast!" Mother called from the hallway.

"Kathryn!" she shouted my name aloud one more time. This time, her voice stirred me to action and put life into my tired body.

When I finished dressing, I went to get Sarah. She was dressed and already had her backpack slung over her shoulder. On our way to the kitchen, we heard mother calling us again, "Sarah! Kathryn!"

"We're coming," I replied.

"Just toast and juice, please!" I said as we entered the kitchen and got settled at the table.

"Same for me, Mom," Sarah chimed in.

"What? No waffles?" Mother asked. Sarah usually ate waffles.

"No thanks," Sarah replied.

We ate our toast and drank our juice in a hurry. The air was filled with excitement. Both of us were eager yet nervous with anticipation on the first day of school. We gathered up our things and headed for the door.

"Good-bye!" we called to her as we left the kitchen.

"Good-bye. Have a good day!" she said, standing in the doorway watching us.

Outside we waited. The bus hadn't come yet and it was no where in sight.

A few minutes later we finally heard the sounds of the old, cranky bus and saw it coming around the corner and down the street.

"Here it comes," said Sarah.

"Hurrah," I yelled, waving frantically at the bus.

As the bus approached, I recognized the bus driver from the previous year. "It's Diane!" I shouted.

"Kathryn, you're awfully cheerful for someone who didn't want summer to end," Sarah said.

"Who would want summer to end?" I asked, thinking that she loved to be right all the time.

We waited patiently until the bus came to a complete stop.

"Hi, Diane!" I said as soon as the creaky door swung open.

"Hi, girls!" she replied, smiling and full of energy.

On the bus, memories of the familiar smells and sounds returned with a new freshness. I watched Sarah's face turn bright red as she strained, trying to open the window. Some things never change. The school bus windows were still impossible to open.

3

The First Day

"Stay seated, Sarah," Diane reminded her in a serious voice.

Sarah was still fidgeting with her window. She was determined to open the window. Without getting out of her seat, she stretched her arms as far as she could and tried with all of her might to open it before we got to school. With one final push, the window opened slowly, making a horrible screeching sound. "Got it," Sarah shouted triumphantly as she strained to open it all the way.

The bus was at least a block away from the school playground and already I could hear the familiar sounds of children laughing and yelling. Hearing these sounds made me want to rush off of the bus quickly to join them. Sarah was right after all; I was starting to get excited about going back to school.

My eyes were straining, searching here and there trying to locate someone we knew among the hundreds of faces. Sarah was looking for her friends and leaning out the window much too far.

"Stay in your seats until the bus comes to a complete stop!" Diane warned again. Sarah sat back down in her seat. The bus pulled up and stopped in the front of the school.

Yes! I saw them. Haley and Jessica stood near the front door. Where were Linda, Kelsey, and Cassie? Had they already gone inside?

"Haley! Jessica!" I yelled. But they didn't hear me.

I wished that Diane would hurry and open the door. Why was it taking so long?

The door swung open and Sarah was out in a flash. Too late though. No sooner had she gotten off the bus than the bell rang. The playground emptied in seconds.

Sarah waited for me and we went into the school building together. The outside of our school was made mostly of stone like a huge fortress. The inside was painted brilliant yellow which made it seem warm and sunny. It was so big you could easily get lost in the building.

"See you after school Sarah!" I called to her as she went in the opposite direction.

Before I went into the classroom, I inhaled a huge breath of air and then exhaled slowly. I crossed my fingers. Why did I always have butterflies on the first day of school?

Going into the classroom sent chills down my spine. I could see the heads turn and it seemed as though everyone was starring at me.

Once inside, I glanced around the room. My heart was pounding. "Please, let someone I know be in this room," I whispered to myself.

Just then, "Whack!" I was stunned from an unexpected, stinging slap on my back. I gasped for air and having quickly recovered, was ready to face the culprit.

"Hey!" I yelled. Turning around, I found myself face to face with--my best friend Haley.

"Haley!" I shouted throwing my arms up in the

air. "You're in this class?" I asked her.

"Yes, can you believe it?" Haley replied.

Then Jessica appeared out of nowhere. "Jessica, you too?" I said.

"Uh-huh, me too," confirmed Jessica.

I spotted Linda at the windows, and I called to her, "Linda!"

She didn't turn around.

I called her name again, a little louder. This time, she heard me and turned around. Her face brightened as her mouth widened into a grin. She came toward us waving her hands in the air.

"Hurrah!" Linda cried.

"What a year we're going to have!" Haley said.

"Together again!" I said, forgetting for a moment where I was.

"Oh, no, I think that we're in trouble," warned Jessica. "We've been talking too loud."

"But she hasn't even called the class to order," insisted Linda.

Everyone turned to see if the teacher was upset by our noisy chatter. Luckily, our new teacher was busy at her desk and didn't seem to notice us.

We watched her quietly working at her desk, seeming to be unaffected by all the activity in the room or at least not disturbed by it in the slightest.

Suddenly, she raised her head. Her eyes peered over her dark brown horn rimmed eyeglasses with only one of her eyebrows raised as she surveyed the room.

"How did she do that?" Linda whispered as she tried to hold one of her eyebrows while attempting unsuccessfully to raise the other one.

"Shhhh, Linda!" I said, covering my mouth quickly to hold in my laughter.

The teacher still said nothing. But not for long. In a matter of seconds, our new teacher was calling the class to order, "Class, please be seated."

Those still standing rushed to find an empty desk. Everyone was curious to find out more about her.

I watched her as she placed her eyeglasses on her desk and brushed her reddish brown hair out of her eyes with the back of her hand. She had a kind face with laugh wrinkles around her mouth and her eyes were a brilliant emerald green.

Slowly, her head turned observing the students as she waited and watched until everyone in the class was seated. Then she stood up, turned her back to us and began writing on the chalkboard.

"She seems nice," I whispered quietly to Haley.

"I hope so," Haley replied, mouthing the words.

"Teachers are teachers," muttered Linda. Muffled laughter could be heard coming from those sitting closest to her.

Sometimes Linda said the most outrageous things. But I knew that deep down inside she really liked school.

Our new teacher turned around and faced the class. If she had heard Linda's comment, she didn't let on! She had written her name on the chalkboard,

Mrs. McConnell.

"Good morning class. Welcome back to school. My name is Mrs. McConnell but you may call me Mrs. M.," she said softly with a kind smile on her face.

Once attendance had been taken, she announced, "Next, we will have introductions. Think carefully about what you would like to tell the class about yourself or about your summer."

A shudder went through my body at the very thought of talking in front of the class. I glanced around the room. Everyone was probably just as scared as me. I knew that it was silly but I couldn't stop from worrying. Having so many of my closest friends in the class should have made me less nervous but it didn't.

"It's great to be back in school with all of our friends," Haley said softly. Not wanting to be heard by the teacher, she leaned so far towards me she almost fell out of her chair.

"Oops, be careful Haley! And, yes, I'm glad to be back with all of our friends," I whispered, nodding in agreement and thinking that summer ending wasn't so bad after all.

Sitting with all of my friends made being in school worthwhile. I couldn't help but wonder if we would be able to sit next to each other all year. Yet in my heart I knew that having an alphabetical seat assignment was inevitable.

While I was waiting for my turn, my head was filled with questions. What would I say? Who am I? What did I do all summer? Did I really want to share any of this with the class?

The teacher glanced up from her notebook holding a pencil in her hand. She was looking around the room wanting to put a face to the next name on her class list.

Observing her uncertainty, I knew that within a week, all of that would change and she would know each and every one of us better than we knew ourselves!

"Kathryn?" Mrs. McConnell called my name.

I raised my hand slowly so that she could see me.

"Kathryn, please introduce yourself and tell us what you did this summer," she said softly. I replied quickly, hoping that no one would notice that my hands were trembling. I held them tightly together to stop them from shaking.

With my heart beating a mile a minute, I looked directly at the class and said, "Hi, my name is Kathryn! My family went to one hundred museums this summer."

At first there was silence but then the class reacted as if in pain from the mere mention of the word "museum".

Their reaction made me sink deeper into my chair. I was flushed and embarrassed. I became more annoyed by the second as my face continued heating up. The class watched and waited. My mouth was dry and I was in desperate need of water.

Haley whispered, "Kathryn!"

Linda jabbed me in the side with her ruler.

"Ouch!" I cried out, more from having been surprised by the attack than from the pain. Some of the boys in class laughed but I didn't care.

"I'm sad that summer is over but glad to be back with my friends at school!" I continued.

My back muscles tightened and I cringed as a cheer echoed around the room. I touched my face because it was hot. I knew that it must have been beet red and I hoped that no one noticed.

"There goes your recess," Linda whispered.

Slowly, I turned to look up at the teacher. Was I in trouble? Would I be staying in during recess on the very first day of school?

Mrs. McConnell's expression told me that she thought the outburst by the class was inappropriate. She peered over her eyeglasses. Her green eyes were squinting and her forehead was furrowed. "We need to listen quietly during introductions. Remember, it's important to treat others the way you want to be treated," she said so quietly that you almost had to strain to hear her.

Mrs. McConnell took off her eyeglasses and rubbed the bridge of her nose. She thanked me for my introduction. "Kathryn, I'm sure you have a lot of interesting facts from your museum visits that you will share with us later in the year," she said.

"Uh-huh," I replied, sitting up straight as an arrow still digesting what she'd said.

The very mention of the words "share" and "museum" sent terror through my body as her words echoed in my head. At that moment, as hard as I tried I was unable to recall one single, solitary fact from the entire summer.

Luckily, she didn't want me to talk about the museum visits right then and there.

Everyone was as eager as I was to be finished with introductions. And it was obvious that Linda wanted class to end; she had been pointing at the clock for the last ten minutes.

Eventually, the teacher had called on everyone, and introductions were over for yet another school year.

Sounding excited, Mrs. McConnell announced, "After recess, I will introduce our newest class member."

"Newest class member?" Linda mumbled under her breath.

I looked over in Linda's direction, wondering the same thing; who could it be? But it was too late to ask since the bell had rung for recess.

Mrs. McConnell stood at the door as we left the room.

4

Henry?

Once outside, Linda, with her arms reaching for the sky, began shouting, "It's recess!"

Haley, Jessica, Cassie, Kelsey and I joined Linda in celebration. We raced each other to the far end of the playground to meet other friends near the wooden benches.

I was having difficulty keeping up with them. "Wait for me," I called to them.

"Hurry, Kathryn, push it a little faster will you," Linda yelled.

"I'm trying!" I replied, not wanting to be the slowest one in the group.

It was difficult but I caught up to them. Haley waited for me like she always did.

"Not bad," Linda replied with a grin when I reached her.

The sun was shining; there wasn't a cloud in the sky. The weather was uncomfortably hot and humid. Yet, everyone was still in a good mood because we were happy to be together again.

"The new teacher seems nice," I suggested.

"I don't know. She's already got a class pet who gets to be tardy on the first day of school," insisted Linda.

"Who do you think the new class member is?" asked Jessica.

"I don't know," I admitted.

"Who ever this new kid is, why didn't she have to come to school on time like the rest of us?" Linda asked.

"Hey! It could be a boy," yelled Wally who was standing nearby. We chuckled.

"Well boy or girl, who could it be?" Linda asked, glancing back at Wally.

No one had a clue.

The new class member was soon forgotten as we began telling stories of summer intrigue.

Linda told hilariously funny and scary tales of her summer. We laughed so hard that our eyes filled with tears.

After all, Linda was the daring adventurer in our group. She always dazzled everyone's imagination and kept us in suspense with her incredible stories.

"Linda, tell the one about the big bear on your camping trip to Canada!" I suggested. Everyone's eyes lit up.

"A bear?" asked Jessica.

"A real bear?" Haley questioned.

"Sure!" Linda replied. Linda cleared her throat before she began her story. Then she started retelling the "Big Bear Tale".

The bears in her story took on a life of their own. "And the scratching noise that we heard along the outside of the tent wasn't my brother like we had planned. It was a real bear!" Linda shouted with her hands up in the air.

Linda's scary stories could make you tremble with fear and her funny stories could make you laugh until you cried.

The end of recess surprised us because the time had gone by so fast. The class mingled by the door, lingering as they returned from recess, discussing who the new class member could be. We were all curious to meet the new kid.

Mrs. M. stood at the door and waited until we had all returned to our desks.

Everyone was present and accounted for; twenty-four pairs of eyes were watching and waiting for the introduction.

"Class, I want to introduce our surprise class member," she said.

"Finally," said Linda. The anticipation was more than she could stand.

"Well, where is he?" Wally spoke aloud, glancing in Peter and Linda's direction. "Or is it a she?" he added with a wink.

Mrs. McConnell seemed to enjoy Wally's question but stood there saying nothing for a moment.

Linda leaned across her desk insisting, "Who ever it is, is tardy!" Linda wanted our teacher to hear her because she thought it was unfair since she had to come to school on time. Those sitting nearby who heard her comment couldn't help but laugh.

Then Mrs. McConnell called the class to order and the room quieted down. Patiently we sat and waited for the new student to appear.

Before another word was spoken, Mrs. McConnell reached down behind her desk and lifted up a cage.

"A cage?" said Linda, both bewildered and surprised by the sight of it.

"Wow!" said Wally.

Everyone was flabbergasted, especially after seeing what was in the cage. Excitement filled the room with the surprise appearance of a small *animal* . This new class member wasn't what anyone had expected.

"Well, it's definitely not a boy or a girl!" Peter said, directing his statement more to Wally and Linda than our teacher.

"Uh-huh, it's a hamster!" shouted Linda.

Linda turned to Peter and with a gleam in her eye and smile on her face, told him, "Although it still is a male or a female, Peter!"

"Linda!" said Haley, giggling.

"Our first 'class pet' of the year!" said Jessica, nudging Linda who had guessed it out on the playground and didn't even know it. Linda turned red from embarrassment. She gave Jessica the thumbs up sign.

"Does the hamster have a name?" I asked Mrs. McConnell.

Mrs. McConnell took the hamster out of its cage. "Let me introduce Henry, the hamster," she said proudly, holding the little furry creature in her hand. She had taken him out of his cage and was holding him gently in her cupped hands, being very careful not to drop him.

Walking slowly around the room, Mrs. McConnell gave everyone the opportunity to see our new class pet up close. Some of us gently stroked the hamster's furry little body.

Once Mrs. M. had placed him back in his cage, the class discussed student work assignments for the care and feeding of Henry.

What a first day of school! The teachers had kept us so busy that our heads were spinning. We didn't even have any time or any reason to be sad about summer being over, especially not after meeting Henry!

The day ended as quickly as it had begun. Everyone was ready to go home when the bell rang.

Haley waited for the bus with Sarah and me. At the last minute before the bus pulled away from the curb, she yelled, "I'll call if I can come over today!"

"Okay!" I shouted out the window, hoping she could.

5

The "T" word

After school, I waited for Haley to call but she never did. I was disappointed but the afternoon was not a total loss. Sarah and I spent time together talking about classes, friends, and teachers. Both of us agreed that it looked like we were going to have a great school year!

At dinner, our parents asked us all about our first day back at school. I told them about Henry, our surprise class member who was tardy. Sarah also shared some very interesting stories about her class.

They seemed pleased that we were excited about school. "Does this mean that you're both going to do well in school this year?" asked my father.

"We didn't say we liked it that much, Dad," I replied in my usual joking manner.

Sarah thought that it was funny when I joked around with father but her laughter tonight was so loud that it was painful. "Sarah, stop it," I demanded, "I wasn't that funny."

"Okay!" replied Sarah, unable to resist smiling.

"We'll do well in school. Won't we, Sarah?" I said, confident that she would.

He sat back in his chair with a silly grin on his face. What was he thinking? Leaning forward, he said, "We just want you both to do well in school."

Well, at least he didn't single me out!

"Haley's in my class again this year!" I said.

Suddenly, their heads came up, their forks went down and they stopped eating. The mood in the kitchen became almost hushed. They didn't seem very happy about what I considered to be pretty good news.

"Kathryn, I know that Haley is your best friend but sometimes you let her help you too much. You should be able to do more things for yourself at school."

"I know," I replied quickly, wishing that I hadn't said anything about who was in my class. I should have known that they would react that way. It was the same every year.

Father was so predictable. I knew that any minute he was going to say that horrible word. Please, I thought to myself. Don't let him say it. Then he did, he said it! He said the "I" word. Didn't he care at all about my feelings?

"Did you hear me, Kathryn?" Father asked.

"Yes, I heard you, Dad," I replied but I hadn't heard his favorite word. Instead, I blocked it out, refusing to listen when he nagged me.

"Kathryn!" said my father, knowing that I hadn't heard him and that I really disliked the "I" word.

My face was heating up but there was nothing I could do to stop it because it always turned beet red whenever I was embarrassed, nervous or upset.

Trying to keep the peace, mother interrupted, "We just want you to help Haley as well as yourself."

Choking on my words, I begged, "Mom, Please!"

At first, I sat silent, not wanting to talk about it.

But then I tried to explain, "Mom, what could I possibly do to help Haley? She's a great athlete, musician, artist. She's gifted at everything! There's not much that I could do to help her. "

"We want you to help yourself more...," my mother replied.

"My other friends help me too. So what? It makes them feel good to help me. Is that wrong?" I asked her.

Mother didn't seem to have an answer to that question. Everyone began to eat again. Sitting quietly, I couldn't help but wonder why they didn't have more faith in me? Sometimes, I doubted whether they understood me or my world at all? The look on their faces gave them away. They listened but hadn't really heard a word that I had said.

Mother hesitated before she suggested, "There's probably something that you could do to help Haley. You'll think of it when the time comes."

I nodded in agreement. It was much easier than arguing with them.

Had they forgotten that Haley was my best friend. I wanted to be as good a friend to her as she was to me. If I could help her, I would.

Sarah and I did a little bit of homework after dinner and before long it was time for bed and the discussion at the kitchen table had faded. In my heart, I knew that someday, they would believe in me and be proud.

I lay in bed enjoying the peace and quiet of the night, having been drained both physically and emotionally after a very active first day at school. Sleep came quickly.

6

A Broken Leg

When the bus pulled up to the school yard, there was a flurry of activity. Everyone was buzzing with excitement. What a commotion!

"What's going on?" I asked, surprised and puzzled by all of the activity.

Jessica and Linda rushed over and told me that Haley had been hurt.

"What? Haley was in an accident?" I asked. I couldn't believe my ears.

"Uh-huh, she was hurt pretty badly," said Linda.

"What happened?" I asked with a stunned look on my face.

"She was in a bicycle accident," explained Jessica.

"Oh, no!" I could hear myself saying. "Is she all right?"

"I think so," Jessica replied, shrugging her shoulders.

"Mrs. McConnell will know," suggested Cassie.

As we made our way toward the classroom, the bell rang but its sound didn't seem real. Talking along the way, we seemed unaware of the time or of the ringing of the second bell.

I was numbed by the news.

No wonder she didn't come over yesterday after school or call. She couldn't. Now I wished that I had called her.

Inside the classroom, there was a lot of discussion and even some confusion concerning what had really happened. Everyone was talking a mile a minute about Haley's accident. Cassie and Kelsey were both talking at the same time, trying to tell me what they knew about it.

Mrs. McConnell asked everyone to join her in the large group meeting area of our room where we sat on the floor and held informal discussions. Once settled, a hush fell over the room and the class listened attentively as she explained what had happened to her.

"Haley was in an accident yesterday after school," she said. A rush of nausea crept over my stomach in seconds. "She was riding her bicycle. And Haley has broken her leg. It is a pretty bad break, a compound fracture." The class reacted with sighs and groans when Mrs. McConnell told us.

"Ooooh! A compound fracture!" Linda said without thinking. "Ouch!"

"Yes, Linda. It does sound awfully painful," Mrs. M. remarked upon hearing Linda's reaction.

Mrs. McConnell continued with the story, "Haley and her sister were out for a ride in the park. Haley lost control of her bicycle after she hit a bump in the road. Her bicycle probably picked up speed as she went down the hill and it flipped over sending her flying through the air near the bottom of the hill. When she landed, her leg hit a nearby tree."

"Incredible," said Peter.

"But she's so good on her bicycle!" Jessica told our teacher.

"Sometimes accidents happen when we least

expect them," Mrs. McConnell reminded Jessica.

Raising my hand, I said, "It's a good thing her sister was riding with her."

Everyone agreed.

Linda raised her hand. Mrs. M. looked concerned, knowing by now that Linda could say some pretty unpredictable things, but she called on her anyway.

"I'll bet it took a long time for them to get help in that section of the park," said Linda.

"But Haley's such a good rider. And she knows the park area so well," Kelsey said very quietly.

"Yeah, and she rides there a lot," agreed Cassie.

"It is important to remember bicycle safety," Mrs. McConnell told the class.

"Was Haley wearing her bicycle helmet?" Peter wanted to know.

Linda raised her hand but didn't wait to be called on. She announced proudly, "I always wear my helmet! My father and mother threatened to take my bike away if they caught me riding without it."

"Yes, luckily, Haley was wearing her bicycle helmet, Peter," Mrs. McConnell answered him. Turning to look in Linda's direction, she said, "And thank you for sharing that information about yourself, Linda." Linda looked embarrassed. Then Mrs. M. faced the class directly. "Everyone should wear a safety helmet when riding their bicycle."

"I always have to wear mine," Jessica told Mrs. McConnell who was trying but unable to resist smiling at Linda's comment.

Linda, who had had more broken bones and more scraped knees than anyone I knew, asked the teacher, "Mrs. McConnell, Haley had to really smack into that tree to have broken her leg. Right?"

"Yes, you're correct Linda," Mrs. M. replied.

Thoughts of such a collision made me cringe as

waves of nausea returned. It was a horrifying thought.

We went on to learn about adjectives and nouns during class time but soon found the clock approaching recess time. When the bell finally did ring, we lingered in the classroom for a while talking.

"Girls, you'll have to go outside, I have work to do," Mrs. M. said.

"Okay," Jessica replied.

"Come on, let's go," Linda insisted, always eager to leave class.

Outside the door to our classroom, I suggested, "Hey, let's make Haley a get-well card on the computer in the library instead of going outside."

"Can't," Linda mumbled.

"Why not?" I asked in a whisper.

"Just can't! No one is allowed in the library during recess," Linda replied.

"I know but I thought that we could ask," I said.

"It's a good idea. It's too hot to play outside anyway," Kelsey added.

Jessica nodded her head in agreement.

"And if the librarian says no, what then?" Linda wanted to know.

"Let's wait until she says no," I suggested.

"Okay," Linda agreed reluctantly.

I set off to the library with my friends.

7

The Get-Well Cards

"I knew that she would agree," I said as we watched Mrs. McKinley walking to another section of the library.

"That's because you're always bringing her candy," Linda said, teasing.

"Linda!" I replied. "Be nice."

Jessica, Linda, Cassie, Kelsey and I spent recess in the library. Mrs. McKinley, our librarian, had the computer and the computer programs that we needed to make the card.

After hearing about Haley's accident, she came back with some colored computer paper for us to use to make our get-well card. "If you need me, I'll be in the reference section," said Mrs. McKinley, as she turned and walked away.

"Kathryn, go ahead and turn it on," said Jessica, who used computers but really didn't like them.

"All right," I replied. I turned on the power and located the word processing program that we would use. Everyone seemed amazed at what I had the computer doing.

We argued a little over the design but finally decided to have Jessica and Kelsey, the best writers, work on a poem. Linda and Cassie worked with me on the art.

Linda had little experience using the computer and it wasn't because her parents hadn't tried. Cassie used the computer occasionally but said that she wasn't comfortable using the graphics programs. As an artist, Cassie's medium had always been charcoal and pencil, while my artistic medium was most definitely the computer.

I demonstrated how to use the new software. "If you two used the computer more often, you would really like it," I told them as I passed the mouse to Linda.

"Not me!" protested Linda. "You're a computer wizard, Kathryn," she insisted. "While I'm a wiz on the basketball court and on the softball field."

"Okay," I said, "but if you change your mind..."

"Don't worry. "I won't change my mind. I'm happy just being the coach!" Linda replied.

"Come on Cassie, you're the real artist, go ahead and try it," I said, turning to her. She began cautiously but was drawing beautifully in no time at all. Linda and I both watched as Cassie's drawing took shape.

"Wow, you caught on quickly, Cassie," said Linda.

"Yes, you're a very good artist," I agreed.

When she had finished the graphic art for our card, Linda and I applauded her efforts. It was a beautiful drawing of Haley with a cast on her leg, surrounded by her friends.

Jessica and Kelsey read their poem for final approval.

"Roses are red, you're sick in bed,
Violets are blue, your friends miss you.
Carnations are white, you gave us a fright.
Flowers are swell, so please get well."

Linda, Cassie and I gave it the green light and

Kelsey typed it into the computer.

The poem and picture displayed on the computer monitor looked impressive. "Is it a go? Are we ready to print?" asked Linda.

"Okay," said Kelsey.

Jessica nodded her head in agreement.

"Cross your fingers," I told everyone.

Linda took the card from the printer and beamed with delight as she proudly held it up for us to see. "It came out great," she said.

The librarian came back because of the noise and excitement.

"What a beautiful card," she said, smiling.

"Thanks, Mrs. McKinley!" Cassie responded.

"You're very welcome," Mrs. McKinley replied.

"We're pretty good at this card business, if I do say so myself," Linda said proudly.

On that note, the librarian smiled, excused herself and went back to work in the reference section.

We continued to talk as we sat around the computer table.

"It's good," cried Linda.

"Well, who wants to go over to Haley's after school and take her our get-well card?" I asked.

"I do," said Linda.

"If I don't have singing lessons, I can go," Kelsey explained.

"Let's meet at Linda's at 4:00 P.M., and then go to Haley's house together," I suggested. I knew that my mother would allow me to go alone to Linda's because her house was on my corner less than half a block away.

"Sounds good to me," replied Linda.

"I know that I can be there," Cassie informed us.

"I'll be there if I can," said Jessica. "If I don't have piano lessons."

"Good, then it's settled. We'll meet at Linda's,"

I said.

At that moment, the bell rang. We gathered our possessions and left the library.

Before going into our classroom, we showed Mrs. McConnell the get-well card. "It's a very nice card," she said.

"We're going over to her house after school to give it to her," I told Mrs. M.

"Haley will sure be surprised to see all of us," Linda suggested.

"Yes, Linda. I'm sure that she will be," said Mrs. McConnell with a smile. Then she called the class to order.

8

Telling Sarah and Mom

It had been a long school day and I was glad that it had finally come to an end. I had almost forgotten about Sarah and the bus. Luckily, the bus was waiting for me. As I rushed around the corner of the building, I could hear Sarah calling my name, "Kathryn!"

Sarah saw me but she kept on calling out my name, "Kathryn!"

"I'm coming!" I yelled but she didn't hear me.

Once on the bus, it took me a few minutes to catch my breath. Sarah sat back in her seat and seemed relieved that I was on the bus.

The ride home was anything but quiet. Full of conversation, Sarah asked me a million and one questions about Haley. She was relentless. I told her everything that I knew about her accident.

"I looked for you at recess. Where were you?" Sarah asked.

"We were in the library working on a get-well card for Haley," I explained.

"I should have known you would be using Mrs. McKinley's computer," she replied. "Where is the card? Show me, will you?"

"Sure," I said as I rustled through my backpack to get them. "The class made one too. But it's too big to unroll on the bus."

"It's good," Sarah replied after reading the poem.

Once home, I shared the story of the broken leg with my mother. She was really surprised because Haley was strong, coordinated, and very athletic. "No one at school could believe it either," I told her.

"Haley seems such an unlikely person to have an accident," Mother said, shaking her head. "See girls, you always have to be careful. You just never know."

"We know," I replied quickly. "And besides, Mrs. McConnell went over bicycle safety and first aid at school," I added, hoping that would reassure her.

"Good, I'm glad she did," replied Mother. Then she picked up the telephone and called Haley's parents.

I went to my bedroom to put away my school things. Realizing that I had forgotten to ask about meeting my friends at Linda's, I rushed back into the kitchen. I needed to ask permission but Mother was still talking on the telephone!

"Psssst! I need to talk to you," I whispered, trying to politely interrupt her.

She frowned. "All right, Kathryn," she said, covering the telephone receiver and motioning to me with her free hand. "Just one more minute."

I waited patiently and finally she hung up the telephone receiver. "Mom, why did you talk so long?" I whined, looking at the clock in the kitchen. "I had to ask you something, now I'm going to be late!"

"Late? Late for what, Kathryn? What was it exactly that just couldn't wait?" she questioned me

35

with an irritated look.

"Mom, I'm meeting my friends at Linda's," I told her. "Then we're going to Haley's from her house."

"Oh?" Mother asked. "And who exactly are *we* ?"

"You know: Jessica, Cassie, Linda and Kelsey," I responded. I told her about the get well cards. "All of us are meeting at Linda's to take them over to Haley," I explained.

"Her mother may not want her to have visitors," she replied with a concerned look.

"We aren't going to stay, Mom," I insisted. "We just want to drop off the cards."

I showed her the get-well card made by the class. "And we made this one for Haley during recess. Mrs. McKinley let us use her computer and paper," I explained.

Mother looked at them. "They are very nice," she said, standing there for a moment deep in thought. And just when I thought that she was going to say no, she said, "Okay, you may go."

"Thanks, Mom," I said with a big grin on my face.

"Don't be disappointed if you can't visit with Haley," she warned me.

"Thanks, Mom. I won't be," I was quick to answer.

"Haley will probably be sleeping," she insisted.

"Can I go now?" I asked. Worried that I would miss my friends, I tried to rush her but it didn't work.

"You are going straight to Haley's house after you meet your friends at Linda's. Right?" she quizzed me.

"Yes, Mom!" I answered.

"After you have visited at Haley's house, you are going back to Linda's with all of your friends. Then, after you get back to Linda's house, you are going to come straight home. Correct?" she asked.

"Yes," I replied. She was starting to confuse even me. "I thought that you and Dad wanted me to be more--you know!"

"Yes, but your dad and I still worry about your safety," she replied. She wasn't smiling anymore.

"I've got to hurry or I'll miss my friends," I told her.

"Okay, be careful and be home in time for dinner," she warned.

"Yes, I promise I'll be careful," I replied, making a quick exit.

My mother followed me outside. She stood on the porch just like I knew she would. "Bye," she yelled, waving.

"Bye! I'll be home on time for dinner," I promised.

Making my way toward the corner and Linda's house, I could feel her eyes watching me. I knew that she wouldn't go back inside until she thought that I had safely reached Linda's front door.

9

Going To Haley's House

Up the street I hurried, huffing and puffing along the way. I moved as fast as I possibly could. I was worried that I might have missed them. We said that we would meet at 4 o'clock and it was already past 4 o'clock.

Then I realized why they couldn't leave without me. I had the cards! How could I have forgotten?

At the corner, I saw Jessica. She was standing on the front porch. Cassie and Kelsey were talking to Linda's mother. And Linda was throwing a baseball with her younger brother in the yard.

"Hey, Jessica, I'm glad you didn't have piano," I shouted. They heard me and started waving wildly.

"Kathryn!" yelled Kelsey.

"No singing lessons Kelsey?" I called to her.

"Not today," she shouted back.

"Thanks for waiting for me," I said when I reached them.

"We were getting worried," Linda said, walking toward me.

"Sorry, I'm late," I told them when I reached the porch. "My mom was talking to Haley's mom on the telephone."

"Haley will be surprised to see all of us," I said.

"Let's get going!" Jessica suggested.

"We're out of here, Mom," said Linda. "Bye, John. Thanks for the game."

Each of us said good-bye to Linda's mother and her brother as we left. We had to hurry to catch up with Linda who was already halfway up the street.

"Come on Linda, wait for us!" I yelled.

"I'm glad we could all go to Haley's," Kelsey said.

"Uh-huh," added Jessica who was busy chasing Linda.

"I thought that I was going to have to baby-sit!" Linda shouted to us over her shoulder while making a face that caused everyone to laugh. We all knew that she never liked baby-sitting.

"Do you think that we'll get to see her broken bones?" Linda asked, ignoring our laughter but slowing down a bit so that we could catch up to her.

"Linda! Only you would want to see the blood and guts," I said.

"I'll get sick if I see any blood or bones," cried Cassie.

"What?" Linda asked, "Why?"

"Because blood makes me faint!" Cassie replied.

"Well, nurses and doctors don't get sick," Linda offered as proof that there was no reason to get ill.

Cassie just shook her head and covered her ears so she couldn't hear Linda.

"Don't worry. Linda's just kidding you. We won't see any bones or blood," I said to reassure her. Besides, I was sure that Haley would have a cast on her leg.

Jessica tried to run ahead of Linda, who was a better runner. They were neck and neck as they approached Haley's house. Somehow, Jessica managed to reach the front porch a split second before Linda. She squealed with happiness at her narrow victory.

"Hurrah!" Jessica said triumphantly, bending over trying to catch her breath.

Linda didn't appear to be tired a bit. She rang the doorbell just as the rest of us reached the porch.

Haley's mother opened the door. She seemed very surprised to see all of us. "Good afternoon, girls," she said.

"We have a get-well card for Haley," I told her, holding it up.

"And we came to visit her!" Kelsey added.

Linda asked, "Can we see her? And give her the card."

"I'm sorry girls but she's asleep and can't have any visitors today," her mother explained.

Our disappointment must have been obvious from the looks on our faces. I handed Haley's mother the cards. "Thank you girls!" she replied.

"You're welcome," I said along with the others.

"Did Haley have any bones sticking out through her skin?" asked Linda.

Cassie yelled, "Linda!"

Linda always said what was on her mind!

Haley's mother stood in the doorway listening. It was as if she couldn't make up her mind about something. And just as we turned to leave, she asked, "Would you girls like a snack?"

It didn't take but a second for all of us to answer "Yes!"

Pangs of hunger made it impossible for us to resist her offer of a snack.

"You will need to be quiet when you come in the house because Haley is asleep," she said softly.

"We promise," I whispered.

"We'll be quiet," Linda agreed.

"Come on in," Haley's mother replied as she opened the door wide and held it until we were all in the house. We rushed in, waited in the hallway and then followed her into the kitchen.

She brought a tray of fruit and cheese along with drinks over to the table. It was more than enough for an afternoon snack.

Before leaving the kitchen, we asked when Haley would be returning to school. Her mother wasn't really sure. "Haley might be home with her leg up in the air for four weeks," she explained.

"That's a long time," I said disappointed.

"I'd enjoy the time off from school!" Linda insisted.

"But Linda, we just started," Cassie said.

At the front door, everyone thanked Haley's mother for the delicious snacks.

"You're very welcome. And thank you for bringing the get-well card for Haley," she replied.

"Tell Haley that we'll be back," I said.

"And that everyone misses her," added Jessica.

Linda grinned, saying, "Especially our new teacher!"

On the way home, we took our time, going slowly. We discussed Haley having to stay home for four weeks. It seemed like such a long time to everyone except Linda.

Once we arrived back at Linda's house, everyone said good-bye and rushed to get home in time for dinner.

10

Helping My Best Friend

Coming in the front door, I could hear my mother and father talking about Haley's horrible accident.

"I'm home!" I called from the hall.

"Good, you are just in time for dinner, Kathryn," my mother answered.

Once settled at the table, everyone had questions about Haley and her accident. "You were right, Haley was sleeping," I told mother. "We didn't get to see her."

"Kathryn, did her mother tell you girls that Haley won't be going back to school for four full weeks?" Mother asked.

"Yes, " I replied.

"Her parents are worried about her going back to school because her leg needs to be kept elevated."

"I know!" I said.

Meanwhile, mother placed a plateful of food in front of me. I stared at it, knowing that I wouldn't be able to eat everything on it. I wasn't hungry, just tired; it had been a long day. I pushed the food around on my plate with my fork, trying to make it look like I was eating.

Eating another morsel of food was difficult but I forced myself, knowing how upset my parents got when they cooked a meal that no one ate.

Suddenly, an idea popped into my head out of nowhere. A way that I could help Haley. I could hardly wait to shout it out. Wouldn't they be surprised.

"Mom and Dad, I have this terrific idea. It is something that I can do for Haley," I declared.

"What?" Sarah asked me.

Both of my parents looked at me and asked, "What do you have in mind?"

Anxious for them to agree, I explained slowly and carefully, "I want to share something very special with Haley. It's something only I could share."

Sarah interrupted, asking, "Share what, Kathryn?"

I looked directly at them and continued, "And Haley could come back to school sooner."

"How?" asked Sarah.

"Get to the point, Kathryn," my mother said.

"Haley could borrow my old wheelchair!" I told them proudly.

"Wow! Haley use your wheelchair!" said Sarah. "What a great idea."

My parents were definitely surprised by the idea. I could see it in their faces. They looked at each other and put down their forks.

After listening, talking and thinking carefully, they replied, "Well, you've got a good idea, Kathryn. Yes, you can let her borrow your old wheelchair."

"All right!" I yelled.

"But we will have to talk to her parents first," they explained.

"When? When will you talk to them?" I asked

impatiently.

"We'll call later, after dinner when the dishes are washed and put away," Mother said.

"Thanks," I replied.

Sarah and I liked to talk when we did the dishes. That night we had a lot to talk about.

"I bet you never thought that I'd be sharing my old wheelchair with Haley, did you?" I asked Sarah.

"That's for sure!" Sarah replied.

"Do you think her parents will agree to let her use it?" I quizzed her.

"Sure, why not?" Sarah said.

When we'd finished, Sarah left the kitchen quickly before mother could think of another job for us to do.

"Mom, we're finished! Now will you call?" I pleaded.

"Yes," she said.

Patiently, I waited listening to her every word. "Mom, did they say yes?" I interrupted her when I could wait no longer.

"Yes, Kathryn!" she mouthed the words.

I couldn't stop grinning. We would be wheeling around school together, both of us using wheelchairs! "All right!" I shouted aloud.

"Shhhhhh," Mother said, motioning me to be quiet with her finger to her mouth.

"Mom, when will we take it over to her house?" I interrupted again.

Getting aggravated, my mother put her hand over the telephone and whispered, "Kathryn, you and your father will take the wheelchair over tomorrow! Now please stop interrupting me."

"Okay," I said, turning to leave.

"Sarah!" I called, rushing down the hall toward her room. "Sarah! She's going to borrow my old wheelchair," I yelled, smiling from ear to ear.

"Haley at school, in a wheelchair just like you, Kathryn!" Sarah said with a smile.

"Can you believe it?" I asked, "It will be such fun."

"What a sight the two of you will be!" Sarah replied. "You're going to turn a lot of heads and surprise a lot of people!"

"I guess so," I said. "Sarah would you help me clean my old wheelchair?"

"Sure," she said.

Off we went to get my other wheelchair. "I can't believe it, can you?" I asked her again.

"Honestly, it sure isn't something I ever imagined Haley doing," Sarah told me.

"I'm glad her parents agreed to let her borrow it," I told Sarah, reaching down to check the tires.

Sarah worked along side me cleaning and checking the wheelchair. After a while she stood back and gave the wheelchair the once over. "Yes, it looks brand new."

"Do you think that Haley will be excited," I asked again.

"I think so," Sarah responded.

When we had finished, it really did look new. I thanked Sarah for helping.

"You're welcome," Sarah replied as she climbed into the wheelchair. "I'll check it out for you."

I watched as Sarah wheeled out of the room and down the hall. How different she looked sitting in the wheelchair, wheeling instead of walking. And I wondered what Haley would look like.

11

The Cast!

The next day after dinner my father and I took the wheelchair over to Haley's house. When we got there, he unloaded my wheelchair first and helped me into it. I raced ahead while he was busy getting the other wheelchair out of the car.

Leaning forward, I was just about to ring the door bell when the door flew open. Haley's mother stood there smiling. "Go on in, Kathryn. Haley is in the family room," she said. "I'll help your dad."

"Thanks," I replied, moving past her in the direction of the family room. Haley was waiting patiently, sitting in her dad's favorite chair. The shades were all up and the room was bright and cheerful with the sun shining in.

As I wheeled toward her, I saw it but I couldn't believe it. My eyes must be playing tricks on me I thought. It was the biggest cast I'd ever seen.

"Wow!" I said. "Now that's what I call a cast!"

Her leg was propped up on top of a huge pile of pillows. She looked up and with a sparkle in her eyes smiled.

"I'm glad you're finally here," she said. "I waited all day for you to come." Haley had the look of mischief on her face.

"Me, too," I replied, staring at her cast. "Haley, the cast on your leg is huge!"

I was impatient for my father to bring in the other wheelchair. I kept glancing toward the doorway wondering why it was taking him so long.

"Where could he be," I said aloud, knowing that he was probably still putting it together outside.

"I knew it was you when I heard the car drive up," Haley said.

"Sorry we didn't get to see you yesterday," I told her.

Haley explained that she had slept most of the day but that her younger brother had told her all about our visit. "The get-well cards are great. Thanks," she said.

"You're welcome," I replied. I told her that we used Mrs. McKinley's computer in the library. Haley asked lots of questions and told me she wished that she didn't have to stay at home.

"Tell everyone thanks," said Haley. "And what's Mrs. McConnell like?"

"She's pretty nice," I admitted.

"Everyone misses you at school," I told her.

"I miss all of you," Haley replied.

After seeing Haley, it was obvious that she was well taken care of inasmuch as she was comfortably set up to watch television with pillows under her feet, under her arms, and even pillows holding up her head.

"Wait until Linda sees your cast, all of these pillows, and the candy."

"Wow! What comfort!" I said, smiling. There were trays on either side of her chair. One had books, paper and pencils while the other had snacks and treats. "What a life!"

"Pretty good, huh?" Haley said with a silly grin on her face. "My parents can't help it if they love me.

47

Kathryn, go ahead and eat something."

"Which one should I try, " I asked her.

"They're all good!" Haley replied.

"Good, I'll try them all!" I announced happily, as I popped a chocolate caramel into my mouth and began to chew. "Mmmm....delicious!" I mumbled with my mouth full.

"Wait until everyone at school sees your cast. It's very impressive. In fact, it's the biggest cast that I've ever seen," I told her. "No wonder your parents are pampering you!"

"Haley, give me a pen, will you?" I asked.

"Pen?" Haley questioned me with a puzzled look, "What for?"

"To sign your cast, silly," I explained. " You don't want the cast to be all white and clean looking when you go back to school, do you?"

"Oh, no! Definitely not! Please, sign it!" she answered already reaching over to grab a pen.

I signed her cast with my name and a picture. "You can't write on some of the new casts. The plaster ones, like you have, are the best."

"I didn't know that," she replied.

"How long before you can come back to school?" I asked.

"I'm not sure, but using your wheelchair means I can go back sooner," she explained.

"I'm glad," I replied.

12

Not Just Any Old Chair!

Finally, I heard my father talking to Haley's parents in the hallway. He was showing them how to take the wheelchair apart and how to put it back together. It would take a while for them to figure that out. I turned my attention back to my friend who was giving me some vivid replays of the accident.

"I'd biked along that path many times and never had trouble," Haley explained. "The land was rocky and bumpy with bushes and trees which can be dangerous for bikers."

After hitting the bump in the road she lost control of her bike and picked up speed going down the hill. "It seemed like one second I was on the bike path and then I was flying down the hill. I ended up laying next to a tree with my bicycle on top of me," she retold the story with such realism.

"Oh," I responded, barely audible. "It sounded awful the first time I'd heard the story. It still sounds pretty bad."

"I was really frightened even though it didn't hurt right away," said Haley.

"You must have been in shock!" I suggested. Her mind must have blocked out the pain I thought as I listened to her every word. She was so descriptive that a rush of nausea swept over me as it had at school the day before.

"At the hospital, that's when it started to really hurt," Haley said. She told me about seeing the doctors, getting x-rays, and having her leg set!

"Ouch!" I replied "I hope I never break my leg!"

"It's really hard not being able to walk," Haley said, explaining that for the last few days she hadn't been able to get anything for herself without asking for help. "And my brother won't always help," she added.

"I know what you mean," I replied. "Sarah doesn't always do everything that I ask her to do either."

"Imagine my brother and your sister jumping to attention when we called them!" Haley said.

"I don't think so," I responded, shaking my head with certainty. Then we both broke out into laughter at the thought of it. "The wheelchair should make it easier for you to get around at home and at school," I told her.

"I'm lucky that you have one that I can borrow," Haley replied.

"Last night, I kept waking up and falling asleep all night long dreaming about your wheelchair," Haley said.

Surprised that she was dreaming about my wheelchair, I listened.

Looking very serious, she confided, "You know that I've never used a wheelchair before, don't you?"

"Yes," I replied. "I know."

"But I've never, ever used one!" Haley insisted.

"Well, it's easy. You'll like it and you'll be an expert in no time at all," I said trying to reassure her.

"I hope you're right," she replied. "Besides, it's not any old chair. It's your wheelchair."

"Using my wheelchair will be easy, Haley," I told her again.

"But Kathryn, you are so good at wheeling around," she insisted.

I couldn't help but smile. "Haley, you'll be good too," I told her. "You'll do fine."

"Kathryn, can I tell you something else?" she asked me.

"Sure! You can tell me anything," I replied.

"Well, I'm afraid. I don't know why, but I am," Haley confessed.

I thought for a moment before I answered her. "I think that it's normal to be nervous. I was anxious when I got my first wheelchair."

"You? You were afraid?" Haley replied.

"Honest," I said, "I was."

She still looked concerned.

"I'll be there to help you, if you need me. Don't worry," I told her.

We were distracted by the sounds of our parents as they made their way into the room with the wheelchair. My father moved the wheelchair right over to Haley.

"Are you ready?" Haley's parents asked her.

"Oh yes!" she answered. "As ready as I'll ever be."

Haley's father reached down and picked her up and placed her in the wheelchair. Then he carefully adjusted her broken leg. We watched her for a moment longer before the silence was broken.

"Well! What do you think?" I questioned her.

"It's all right," Haley responded tentatively.

"Are you comfortable?" her mother asked.

Haley looked a little overwhelmed by it all. "Well, it's different," she said, bending over to check out the wheelchair brakes that she had seen me use many times.

"Looks like it will be fun to wheel around in that," her father said.

"Uh-huh," Haley said, shrugging her shoulders. She didn't know what else to say. I understood. I waited, watched and listened, ready to answer any questions that she might have.

"You seem comfortable in the wheelchair, Haley," her mother said.

"The seat is padded. It's nice," Haley replied. Then she began fidgeting with the wheelchair, really checking it out. She started to maneuver it, turning left then right and then left again. Moving around she realized that it was possible to do a lot more than she first thought.

Haley ventured out into the hall, turned around and came back into the family room. Haley looked up at all of us, smiled and said, "Wow! At least now I can get around downstairs!"

"And where did you get this special leg rest for the wheelchair?" she asked, "It works great!"

"Yeah, it's pretty good," I said.

Her father interrupted, "It will hold your leg in different angles. If your leg is elevated, it will heal faster because that will prevent fluids from collecting there. The doctor will let you know how much to raise it up."

Haley was turning around in the wheelchair and didn't seem to be listening to him. "Uh-huh! Whatever you say, Dad," she replied half listening. But her father didn't hear her either; he was already half way into the kitchen.

"Good! They're talking again, Haley. I'll be able to stay and visit as long as they keep talking," I said.

"Kathryn, why do you have this special leg rest attachment thing for your wheelchair?" Haley asked.

"A few years ago, I had surgery on both of my feet and calves," I told her.

"I didn't know that you had surgery, Kathryn. Was it awful?" Haley asked.

"Yeah! Just thinking about it gives me the shivers," I said.

"How long ago was it?" she quizzed me further.

"I was little when I had the surgery. I had to keep both of my legs up in the air to prevent swelling," I told her.

"Wow. Sounds horrible! Both legs?" Haley asked.

"It wasn't too bad. Anyway, that was when we got the attachments for my wheelchair," I replied.

We sat quietly for awhile. My surgery was something that I had never talked to anyone about. Now I had confided in my best friend. I was glad that I had told her about it because I knew she cared. She was always nice to me from the very first day I met her at school.

"Was the surgery done so you could walk?" she asked softly.

"No," I answered quickly. I tried to change the subject, but she didn't give up easily.

"Never? You'll never ever be able to really walk?" Haley questioned me.

"Haley, I will never be able to really walk. With work, I will be able to walk with crutches or a walker for short distances but not 'walk' as you know it," I explained. My stomach was getting a little queasy again.

Haley's forehead turned into a frown, "Oh," she replied in her softest voice.

"Haley, don't look so sad. Smile, will you!" I said. I touched her gently on the shoulder, wanting to let her know that it was all right that I couldn't walk.

We sat quietly for a few moments.

"Kathryn, when the doctor decides what day I can come back to school, I'll call you right away," she said.

"Don't worry about a thing. On your first day back, I'll find you as soon as I get to school. I'll show you everything that I know about wheelchairs," I promised her.

"Thanks, Kathryn!" she replied.

"Kathryn! Let's go," my father said, peering into the room on his way down the hall toward the front door.

"I've got to go Haley," I told her.

"Thanks for coming to visit," Haley said. "And for letting me use your wheelchair!"

"Coming Dad," I called out to him as I wheeled out of the room.

Near the door I stopped, twirled around and said, "Haley, I'll be back to visit again as soon as I can."

"All right!" Haley cried. "Thanks again."

My father was waiting and getting impatient. His foot tapping gave him away every time. He held the door for me as I wheeled under his arm. My mouth curved into an wide grin as I thought about my mother; she would have made me open it myself. Sometimes it was nice to have help.

"Good bye, Haley," I yelled to her from the front porch.

"Good bye, Kathryn," she shouted back to me.

On the drive home, I told him, "Thank you for letting me share my old wheelchair with Haley."

"You're welcome," he said, never taking his eyes off the road.

"Haley was really excited about the wheelchair, don't you think?" I asked.

"She seemed to be," he replied.

"Haley really needs me now because no one at our school knows how to use a wheelchair except for me. She's going to need my help," I told him while studying his face for a reaction.

"Yes, I think you're right, Kathryn," he replied matter-of-factly.

"She's my best friend," I said proudly.

"I'm glad she has a friend like you, Kathryn," he said.

If my father remembered the "I" word conversation we had after the first day of school, he never showed it. And I wasn't about to bring it up. It was insulting enough that they thought I didn't do anything by myself when I did.

The rest of the ride home was quiet.

13

Not Quite Ready For Wheelies

While I was visiting Haley after school a week after the accident, her mother came into the family room and excitedly asked, "Did Haley tell you the good news, Kathryn?"

"No? What good news?" I said shaking my head. I turned and looked directly at Haley. She had been very quiet all afternoon which wasn't like her at all.

"Haley, tell me!" I said eager to know what it was.

"Tomorrow's the big day," Haley replied, "I'm going back to school."

"All right!" I cheered. "You're coming back to school!"

Haley just sat there quietly. She didn't seem to be happy about the news. "What's the matter? Aren't you glad about coming back?" I asked her.

"Sure," Haley responded, "but I am nervous about getting around school in the wheelchair."

"That's all? You're just worried about wheeling around in the wheelchair?" I asked.

"I guess so," Haley answered.

"Well, don't worry about a thing," I said. "I promised that I'd help you and I never break a promise.

"Thanks," Haley said as her frown slowly disappeared. We didn't talk about it again that day.

At school the next morning, Haley arrived shortly after I did. I didn't forget. And when she arrived I was waiting on the sidewalk with Sarah standing beside me.

"Haley!" I shouted as soon as the car stopped. Sarah joined in calling her name. Haley smiled and waved when she saw us.

"Hi, Kathryn. Hi, Sarah," Haley yelled out the window.

The car door swung open and she peered out of the car. We waited patiently for her mother to reassemble the wheelchair. Haley seemed a little flustered but I knew she would be fine once she got used to wheeling around.

"Be careful of my leg," Haley whined as her mother lifted her into the wheelchair.

"What a cast!" squealed Sarah who was standing beside me.

"You look great, Haley," I said.

"Welcome back!" Linda shouted.

"We'll take good care of her," I told her mother. We all said good-bye to her mother, then turned and went into the building.

The corridor was filled with an uncomfortable silence as we began wheeling down the hall to our class. Heads turned. People stared.

A small group of kids followed us as we wheeled through the halls. Their chatter could be heard as they whispered softly to one another. Some didn't know why Haley was in the wheelchair.

"I'm back," Haley called out to the principal who

was walking toward us.

"Welcome back, Haley," Principal Oakley said.

"Nice cast!" she took her pen out of her pocket and asked, "May I sign your cast?"

"Sure," Haley replied.

We watched as she bent over and signed her name. She looked up when she finished and said, "Have a good day." We told her we would and watched as she disappeared around the corner.

As we entered our classroom, a hush fell over the room. Everyone observed us closely as we wheeled into class trying desperately to maneuver around the desks and chairs.

"Wow! Two wheelchairs!" Peter shouted with his arms waving wildly in the air. Then commotion and bedlam erupted like it did when we first met Henry.

"Welcome back, Haley!" Our classmates called out to her.

"Yeah, welcome back," Jessica bellowed, giving her the thumbs up sign.

"We missed you!" Kelsey shouted.

Haley wheeled around the room bumping into everything. "We can hardly move around in here," she complained. But she seemed happy to be back. I knew that she was nervous but no one else could tell and the room would seem a lot bigger once she got used to moving around.

"You're pretty good at wheeling," yelled Kelsey.

"Thanks," said Haley blushing before getting stuck between two desks.

Linda, Cassie, Jessica, Kelsey and I were by her side as she went past all of the curious eyes.

"Don't stare!" Linda shouted.

"I'm seeing double!" yelled Wally, laughing with Peter.

"You'll get double the trouble, if you don't stop,"

Linda warned them.

I realized it was a shock for everyone to see both of us in wheelchairs in the same classroom.

In the meantime, Mrs. McConnell walked back into the classroom. She saw us and came over right away. She was concerned and wanted to know if Haley was feeling all right.

"Yes, Mrs. McConnell. I feel great," Haley replied, "I'm glad to be back in school."

"We will do our best to make you feel comfortable," Mrs. McConnell explained. Then she apologized for not having a desk for her that the wheelchair could fit under like mine.

Listening to Mrs. McConnell's explanation about not having the right kind of desk triggered frustrating memories of my first years at school without a desk or computer or books on audio tape.

Mrs. McConnell turned back toward the class after talking with Haley. She took the attendance and the lunch count.

I sat quietly remembering. I was the first person to ever go to our school who used a wheelchair. Now with Haley, there would be two of us using wheelchairs at school. What a week we were going to have.

At first, things would be a little hectic. I knew that it would take everyone time to get adjusted. Before I came to our school, the teachers, parents and kids thought if you used a wheelchair you had to go to a special school.

Some kids who use wheelchairs do go to special schools. I did for a while and it helped me learn to do a lot of things by myself.

My mother worked hard to change people's attitudes so I could attend my neighborhood school with my sister. But I was the one who had to go to school. I had to make it on my own. It wasn't easy!

"I wish the bell would ring soon," Haley whispered in my ear.

"Me too," I replied. I could hardly wait for recess, just to be on the playground together in wheelchairs.

Where to start? What would I show her first? Just wheeling around together on the playground would be great. It was as though a new chapter in my life was about to begin.

We heard the bell ring and our eyes lit up. Both of us were excited and eager to get outside so we could wheel around.

"Come on Haley," I called to her, "Hurry!"

I waited for her by the door. She poked along slowly because she wasn't used to the wheelchair.

"Okay, I'm coming. I'm not very good at this you know. I'm not quite ready for wheelies!" she cried.

"You're doing great," I replied.

Once out on the playground, I began to demonstrate how to hold one wheel and turn the other in order to go in another direction. Haley tried but it seemed a little frustrating for her at first.

We started slowly on the flat areas of the playground, wheeling everywhere that we could. We wheeled around corners, across the grass, on the sidewalk areas, forward and backward. We tried easy turns and hard turns.

"You were right, Haley!" I shouted.

"Huh? Right about what?" she asked me.

"You're not quite ready for wheelies!" I told her.

Haley smiled but said nothing.

"Getting tired?" I asked her.

"No way," Haley answered.

As we approached a sidewalk with a steeper incline, I stopped.

"Let's practice using the brakes," I said, smiling.

"Miss Martin, my physical therapist is always saying, 'Wheelchair safety is important'."

"Good idea," she replied. "I want to make sure I can stop."

Haley did quite well using her brakes on the hills.

"Let's go over there," said Haley, pointing with her leg. She wasn't tired even after wheeling up some of the steeper ramps at school. But I was beginning to breathe heavy. It was a lot of work, all of this wheeling. She was wearing me out, but I would never tell. I couldn't help but be impressed with her strength.

As we wheeled around, a small group of little kids started to form a circle around us. They had been watching us for quite a while and they finally got the courage to come up to us.

They asked Haley why she was in the wheelchair. She explained to them that she'd broken her leg. They listened and then went back to playing without a word.

It was nice not being the one answering all the questions for a change.

Irritated by all of the attention, Haley said, "I don't like it when they stare. How many times do I have to tell them I broke my leg?"

I told her, "Probably a lot of people today, fewer people tomorrow and even less the day after. People will always stare or ask why."

"Oh," Haley said calmly.

After a few minutes, Haley asked, "Kathryn, I guess you're used to having people stare at you, huh?"

I laughed. "Yeah, I guess so," I replied, trying to think if there was ever a day that went by when someone didn't stare. "Yes, people love to stare. Some ask why you're in a wheelchair, and others don't," I explained, "They're just curious."

"You know, I used to watch you in the wheelchair. I thought it might be fun to use one, but it's not fun for very long, is it?" asked Haley.

"Haley, it's only your first day back," I said.

"Thanks," Haley replied, sitting taller in her chair and looking proud of herself. "Kathryn, you're right. It is only my first day back at school!"

"That's the spirit," I told her.

From experience, I knew as the days went by, Haley would become less self-conscious about being in a wheelchair. She would become less upset when asked "why?". And soon, Haley would become quite good at using the wheelchair and answering questions.

After recess we wheeled back into class and prepared for science. Haley whispered, "I'm getting pretty good. Don't you think, Kathryn?"

"Not pretty good, really good!" I replied, meaning every word.

"Better watch out during lunchtime recess," Haley warned.

"We'll see," I said jokingly.

14

Good News and Bad News

With volcanic eruptions being the topic for the day, science was explosive. Everyone wore plastic safety goggles. Science was my favorite subject and it went by faster than any other class.

When lunch time arrived, we were glad because it was going to be a new and different experience with Haley being in a wheelchair. We were hungry and our growling stomachs proved it.

Looking concerned, as she glanced around the cafeteria, Haley asked, "How are we going to get our lunch trays to the table? I don't think we can do it. How can both of us carry the trays with our drinks, wheel the wheelchairs, and save a table? And won't the tables be gone when we finally get there?"

I listened to all of her questions and concerns until she was finished, then I tried to reassure her, "Haley, don't worry. We'll do it!"

Haley's brow became more relaxed but she still wasn't convinced. "Really, Kathryn. It's too difficult! The tray is too wobbly," she said, demonstrating her concerns.

"You're right. It's difficult to move the wheelchair and balance the lunch tray at the same time!" I agreed.

Trying to look very serious, I said, "Haley, there's good news and there's bad news!"

"What's the bad news?" she asked.

"The bad news is no matter how difficult it is, if we have to do it, then we'll do it," I answered.

"Okay, then what's the good news?" she asked.

"Well, the good news is that if we need it, people are always willing to help," I replied.

"Great idea, let's ask for help!" Haley suggested.

Waiting in the lunch line, I told her, "Just in case I'm sick this week or next, and you have to do it alone, I'll show you how to do it."

Haley looked at me puzzled and asked, "Carry all of this to the table while wheeling?"

"Be patient. As soon as we get our milk, I'll show you what I mean," I told her. "Then you'll be prepared if you are all alone." I was surprised because I was sure Haley had seen me do this before.

"How many milks today, Kathryn?" the cafeteria worker asked.

"One white milk, please," I replied. Usually, I bought three milks at lunch.

"Only one?" she asked surprised.

"Yes. Just one," I replied. "Thanks."

I turned to Haley after she had gotten her milk and said, "Okay, we've got our milk. Now watch me. Haley are you listening? Pay attention and watch carefully. Hold the milk carton by the top. Put it between your teeth."

Getting ready to try it, Haley asked, "In my mouth? Hold it between my teeth?"

"Yes!" I replied. "Now place your food tray in your lap, like this," I mumbled with the milk carton in my mouth.

Haley wasn't smiling.

"You need your hands free to wheel, Haley," I said, as I continued demonstrating my technique. "Then wheel! Just wheel, but wheel quickly to the table before you drop something."

Haley stared at me with raised eyebrows and eyes bulging out of their sockets. "What?" she asked "Kathryn, are you pulling my leg?"

"No," I told her. "Don't you remember ever seeing me do this?"

"No!" she replied.

"Well, sometimes I do get my own lunch you know," I said being serious.

"Okay, but this is just in case I'm alone. Right?" Haley demanded to know. Her big, curious eyes begged for the truth.

"I'm just showing you, so you will know how to do it!" I said.

"Oh," Haley said. "Our friends are going to help us. We don't need to worry about carrying the lunch trays, the drinks or saving the table, not today anyway," I replied, trying to boost her confidence.

"Good!" she replied.

"It's nice to have people help when we need it," I said. "You always save a seat for me and help to carry my tray."

"Yes, I guess so," Haley said softly.

I watched Haley while her head turned back and forth, her eyes searching the crowded cafeteria. "Who are we going to ask to help us with our trays?" she asked me.

Jessica and Kelsey were coming up behind us in line. "Would you come back and help us with our lunch trays," I asked them.

"Sure," Kelsey answered quickly.

While they were getting their food trays and milk, I whispered to Haley, "People like to help."

"You're right again," Haley whispered back to me.

"Sometimes I need help and sometimes I don't. I

do like people to ask me if I need help before they start pushing my wheelchair. It's more polite," I said.

"I'll remember that," Haley said.

Just then Linda came through the line. "Need help with those trays?" she asked.

"Jessica and Kelsey are coming back to help. Thanks for offering," I told her.

"I'll go save the seats at the table for everyone," Linda yelled over the noise in the cafeteria.

"Thanks, Linda," I replied.

Jessica and Kelsey were back in seconds. They each took one of our lunch trays and we followed them to the table. Thank goodness, because it was always difficult getting around the tables in the lunchroom.

"Will you move?" Haley yelled as she ran into the back of Peter's legs.

"Hey, stop that Haley," Peter said angrily.

"Hmmmph," Haley replied, wheeling past him.

Wheeling up beside her, I said, "Haley, do you remember our third grade teacher, Mrs. O.?"

"Uh-huh," Haley asked, bewildered. "Why?"

"Well, Mrs. O. taught me that running into people with my wheelchair to get them to move out of the way was unacceptable. Do you remember?" I asked her.

"I remember you running into me now that you mention it!" Haley said.

"Just say excuse me. It works every time."

"Huh? Oh, I knew that," she replied.

She started saying excuse me and we made it through the maze of people to our table in no time. Now all we needed to do was to get the wheelchairs positioned properly at the table.

"It's stuck! It's stuck!" cried Haley.

I leaned over to look at her wheelchair. "No, Haley. Look at your wheelchair brake. It's locked. You must have hit it accidentally," I said, pointing at the brake on her left wheel.

She reached down to release the brake. "Wow, you're right," she said.

Haley wasn't quite close enough to the table.

"Wait a minute. I'll show you," I said, leaning over to help. I reached over and took off the foot rest. Then I pushed really hard to get the left side of her wheelchair closer to the table.

"It's not close enough," Haley cried, looking distressed.

"It's all right. We'll fix it," I told her.

I leaned over, looked under the table, and found the problem. One wheel was too close to the table leg. "The table leg is in the way," I explained.

By this time, everyone was looking under the table!

"She's right!" shouted Linda.

"Yeah," said Jessica.

"Okay!" I replied.

"Come on, stop fooling around. I'm hungry," said Haley. Haley was moving the wheelchair around trying to get it away from the table leg.

"Haley, the trick is to push in really close even if you start to tilt backwards just a little and then quickly lock the wheelchair," I explained.

"I'm trying Kathryn," said Haley. She was straining and her face was turning red. I could tell that she was getting really frustrated.

Linda jumped up to help. Together with Linda's strength and my direction, we got the wheelchair secured in the right position.

"Thanks," Haley said, relieved.

"Now we can eat!" Linda shouted, with her arms raised to the ceiling. And eat we did!

It seemed like we weren't sitting down for more than a few minutes when the bell rang. "I can't believe the bell rang!" Haley cried. "We just got started." No sooner had Haley finished than the second lunch group began rushing into the cafeteria.

"Lunch period is too short," said Linda with her half-eaten lunch still sitting on her tray.

Just then, Claire and Abby walked by and stopped at our table. "You're really slow pokes today!" they said with good sized grins.

"It's the two wheelchairs!" Linda said, as she jumped up ready to defend us. She was like a firecracker that had gone off. "It takes time to get set up," she said, "especially with two." Linda was furious. She moved closer to them and stood there glaring.

"It's okay, Linda," I said, trying to calm her down. Her face was flush so I knew that she was upset. I hated to see her get into an argument trying to defend us.

"You two can help tomorrow," suggested Jessica, attempting to make peace.

The rest of us all agreed, "Yeah! Great idea!"

"All right, you two can help tomorrow," Linda said with a sneer.

Turning three shades of pink, Claire and Abby replied, shaking their heads, "Sure. We'll help tomorrow. We were only kidding."

"Come on, let's go," Cassie suggested.

"Kathryn, is it time to throw away our trash?" Linda asked with a gleam in her eyes.

I knew we were both thinking the same thing.

"Okay, let's play!" I said, unlocking my wheelchair and picking up my tray and my trash.

"I'll bet you three sticks of gum that I can make a basket from the farthest point," Linda replied with a wink as she proudly held them in the air.

"Wait for me," cried Haley, gathering her tray and trash.

68

After depositing our lunch trays on the assembly line to be cleaned, we headed in the direction of the trash barrels.

"Watch me!" I called to her. I concentrated on my first basket attempt so it would go in. I wanted to win the bet with Linda. Think basket, I told myself.

"Swishhhh!" I made it but I knew I was too close to the trash barrels to be any competition for Linda.

"Lock your wheels first," I told Haley.

She was in position. Her arms went up as her hand held the milk carton in a downward direction. She threw it. The milk carton went sailing through the air, landing right smack in the middle of the barrel. Poof! Swishhhh!

"Good basket, Haley," I said, applauding her efforts.

"Can't beat this one," Linda said, standing even farther away from the barrel. "Swishhh!" Success! Linda's baskets usually went in and she was good from almost any distance.

"No one can beat you, Linda!" I said, handing her the chewing gum. "And don't chew it in class!"

With our trash in its proper place, lunch was officially over!

15

Ready To Go Home

While we were at lunch and recess, Mrs. McConnell rearranged more desks to make room for the two of us with our wheelchairs. One wheelchair was difficult enough in the classroom but now there were two! It seemed like one of us was constantly wheeling into a corner that we couldn't back out of. Earlier in the day, she'd promised us that she would make even more adjustments after school.

"Multiplication and division for review today," said Mrs. McConnell. The class was pulling out their math sheets when we heard Haley and looked up.

"It just won't fit!" Haley cried aloud. She looked angry and aggravated.

"What's the matter?" I asked.

"I can't fit under the desk with this darn wheelchair," said Haley, looking extremely frustrated.

"Wheel in at an angle," I suggested.

"It doesn't work. I can't get close enough to do my work. Now my leg won't fit under the dumb desk," she complained.

The teacher rushed over. The desk problem was not a new one. She stood there trying to think of a solution and said, "Give me a second, Haley. We'll figure something out."

Haley calmed down. She looked more relaxed and seemed confident that Mrs. McConnell would fix everything.

There was only one desk in the classroom, in the whole school for that matter, that a wheelchair could fit under. It was my desk. "Haley can use my desk while she's in the wheelchair," I said, hoping that Mrs. McConnell would let her.

"Kathryn, you need a desk too," Mrs. McConnell said. "But thank you for offering."

I didn't give up. "I really want her to use it, Mrs. McConnell," I said softly, looking her right in the eyes.

Mrs. McConnell apparently saw the sincerity in my eyes and heard it in the sound of my voice. "All right Kathryn, but just for today," she insisted. "Thank you."

"You're welcome," I replied. I was glad she had agreed.

"Are you sure it's okay?" Haley asked.

"Yes, I'm positive. Besides, I don't have my leg up in the air with a cast on it," I reminded her.

"Thanks," Haley replied.

"Okay, girls. Let's do it right away then," Mrs. McConnell said.

With Jessica's help, I moved my supplies and books to Haley's desk. Cassie helped Haley move her things to my desk.

Once we got settled in our new desks, Mrs. McConnell began teaching mathematics. It was one of my better subjects so it went by quickly.

Next, Mrs. McConnell prepared to read aloud to the class. Linda whispered, "I heard Principal Oakley tell Mr. Johnston that Mrs. McConnell was the 'best read aloud teacher' in the whole city."

Once she began to read the story, I knew that our principal was right. Mrs. McConnell's voice was mesmerizing and had almost an hypnotic effect on us.

Suddenly the bell for afternoon recess rang and the class disappeared out the door in seconds. Haley and I took our time. There was no need to rush.

"Do you want to play tetherball?" Haley asked on our way out the door.

"Okay! Let's hurry or the bell will ring before we even get to the front of the line," I told her. Off we went straight to the tetherball area. The lines were long as usual but we waited patiently.

"Look Kathryn, there's Sarah. She's already playing tetherball," Haley said.

Waiting in line for our turn we heard a smack! "Ouch!" Sarah cried. She was hit right in the face with the ball. The sound of the ball as it hit her made me cringe.

Trying to get my attention, Haley pulled on my arm. I turned and asked, "What?"

She looked sick to her stomach.

"Are you feeling all right?" I asked, thinking perhaps the heat and all of the excitement was too much for her. After all, she wasn't used to wheeling around in a wheelchair.

Quickly holding her finger up to her mouth, she motioned for me to whisper. "I don't want to get hit in the face with the ball. How can I play sitting in the wheelchair? I'm too low!" Haley said quietly.

So that was it. I tried to look serious because I didn't want to hurt her feelings. "Don't worry about getting hit!" I told her. "It's really the same as when you're standing up."

I thought about it and realized it would be natural for her to be nervous, especially after seeing Sarah get hit right smack in the face. Not to mention we were lower to the ground, and sitting in wheelchairs. Not having used a wheelchair before, she wasn't as quick or as mobile.

Worried now that she might get hurt, I offered advice.

"Just duck! That's all you have to do. Just duck!" I told her. I crouched over and demonstrated exactly how to avoid getting clobbered by the ball.

"All right, if you say so," she replied, looking nervous.

"If you don't want to play, it's all right," I told her.

"I'll play," Haley replied, taking a deep breath.

"That's the spirit," I cheered.

"I'll just duck," she added, "I'll remember."

Finally, we made it to the front of the line. The game started out pretty slow with Haley gently returning the ball.

Then, halfway through, the game started to gain momentum. Haley forgot about the wheelchair and she started really playing ball. The game got faster and faster.

"You were right. It's easy!" she yelled.

Haley twisted her body to get as much power into the ball as she could. What a hit! The ball kept twirling and twirling. I couldn't reach it.

"Hurrah," chanted the crowd. "What a game!"

Haley really seemed to enjoy it. Now she was confident she could avoid getting hit in the face by the ball.

After our turn ended, she couldn't stop talking about the game. "Wow, that was fun, Kathryn," she said.

"I knew you would be good," I told her.

We were looking for something else to do when we heard screams. It was Linda shouting at the top of her lungs from across the playground.

"Hey, Kathryn! Haley! Come here!" Linda yelled.

Jessica, Cassie and Kelsey joined in with shouts

which could be heard around the entire school yard, "Kathryn! Haley!" they called us.

Linda was waving her arms in the air, yelling, "Wheel those chairs over here! Come on! Move it!"

We glanced at each other, then at Linda and burst into laughter. I yelled, "We're coming!" And we began to wheel over to her.

We had no choice but to go. Linda had that effect on people like no one else I knew.

Wheeling over, I glanced over at Haley, checking to make sure she was doing all right. What a day! It was wonderful to have my best friend to wheel around with at school.

"You two are pretty fast in those wheelchairs," said Linda.

"Thanks," I said with a grin.

No sooner had we reached Linda then the bell rang ending recess. We arrived at our class just in time to become part of another traffic jam in the doorway.

Once in the classroom, we rushed over to get Henry out of his cage until Mrs. McConnell started class.

We ere excited about our new class pet but hadn't had much time to play with him.

"I can't reach his cage," cried Haley.

"I'll get him for you, Haley," offered Linda as she raced across the room.

Linda was at our side in seconds with her arm already inside the hamster's cage. She held him by the thick fur on the back of his neck and lifted him out. Carefully, she handed Henry who was acting a little fidgety to Haley.

Jessica, Cassie and Kelsey gathered around to pat the furry creature. Everyone liked the part of the school day when we could take care of the animals.

Henry looked like he was resting comfortably on

74

Haley's lap when suddenly her face turned bright red, and she had a very surprised look on her face. Something had happened but what?

"Oh, no. He did it!" she cried, looking distressed.

"Did what?" I asked alarmed.

Linda was grinning from ear to ear. "I'll get him, Haley," she said rushing back to her side.

Haley was silent. Linda scooped up Henry and returned him to his cage.

Then we noticed it. The wet spot on Haley's shorts. It was in the exact place that Henry had been sitting.

"Ohhhhhh, no!" I said.

"Ohhhhhh, yes!" Haley replied.

We started to clean up the mess but it wasn't working.

"More paper towels," pleaded Haley. When Linda returned with them, we burst into giggles, laughing so loudly that we disturbed the entire class.

Mrs. McConnell came over to see what all of the commotion was about. She began laughing too. Soon the entire class was laughing.

After a while, everything was back to normal, except for the wet spot on Haley's lap.

It sure had been a long day for Haley. I could see she was starting to get tired. She was even complaining about her leg and that worried me. "It's not as easy as I thought it was going to be," Haley said.

"What?" I asked.

"Wheeling!" Haley replied.

"Wheeling?" I asked.

"Yeah, I thought sitting in the wheelchair would be easy," Haley said, " but it's not."

"I'm exhausted too," I confessed. It had been a long day. "I don't usually wheel around school this much," I admitted.

"So, you have been showing off," Haley said jokingly.

"Well, maybe just a little," I admitted with a chuckle. Noticing how slow she was moving, I told her, "It'll get easier each day."

"I hope so! My arms are too weak to push the wheelchair another inch," Haley replied.

We had had a busy day filled with lots of activity. It was only her first day back at school since the accident. She was happy to be back at school but relieved when the day finally ended. Haley was ready to go home.

16

Elephants and Baby Gorillas

What a week we had at school. Haley had become quite skilled at using the wheelchair! She was even starting to give me pointers.

Now that Haley was stronger, we could go on longer trips. We could hardly wait for Saturday because my parents were taking Haley, Sarah and me to the zoo.

Haley told me, "I have never been to the zoo in a wheelchair! And I'm really looking forward to it."

I tried to tell her it wasn't any different. "It's the same whether you are walking or wheeling," I explained but she didn't believe me. I hoped she wouldn't be disappointed.

Finally, Saturday arrived!

Mother and Sarah loaded the wheelchair into the car while father helped me get into my seat. "Hold on to the grab rail," he said.

"Okay," I replied.

"Thanks for helping me, Kathryn," my father said.

"You're welcome," I said, sitting back and enjoying the wind blowing in my face as we drove away. It seemed like only a few minutes before we were pulling up in front of her house.

When I saw Haley sitting in the wheelchair along with her parents on their front porch, my heart started racing. I was so excited that I thought I was going to burst.

"Hi, Haley!" Sarah and I yelled out the window.

"Hi, Kathryn! Hi, Sarah! I can't wait until we get there," she said excitedly.

"Me, too, " I said.

"Me, three," Sarah said in stitches over her own sense of humor.

We laughed and talked all the way to the zoo.

"We're here!" Sarah shouted when she saw the sign for the zoo.

It seemed to take my parents forever to get our wheelchairs out of the car and reassembled.

"Okay, we're ready," my mother and father called as they came around from the back of the van with the wheelchairs.

Sarah helped to lock my wheelchair as I prepared to get into it. Dad lifted Haley into her wheelchair and helped her get her leg with the cast set up safely on the extender.

"I love the zoo," I told them on the way toward the special entrance for people using wheelchairs.

"It sure is a lot quicker to go through these lines," said Haley.

"The wheelchairs won't fit through the other lines," Sarah informed her. "We've tried it!"

"Haley, what do you want to see first?" I asked her once inside.

"Let's go see the elephants!" Haley suggested.

Sarah agreed.

We were off, wheeling as fast as we could. Sarah ran to keep up with us.

"Watch where you're going," my mother warned.

"We will," we promised her.

Sarah was our unofficial guide. She walked ahead of us and made sure our path was passable.

"This is great," said Haley, "I love wheeling around the zoo instead of walking."

"You sure are strong. You can really push that wheelchair!" Sarah said, after observing Haley wheeling around.

"Thanks," Haley said. "I like using it too."

"There are so many elephants," said Sarah.

"I wonder how they decide which elephants stay outside and which ones go inside?" Haley asked.

"Now that's a good question. Do you want to ask the zoo keeper?" I asked with a chuckle.

"No, Kathryn," said Haley while trying to push me but I got away.

Inside the elephant building, it always smelled the same. It made my nose wrinkle. "It smells like a zoo in here," Haley shouted. Sarah and I started laughing and even my parents were smiling.

"It's dark in here too," I said.

We spent most of our time watching the baby elephants. I was getting tired of being inside. "Let's go see the lions and then the giraffes," I suggested.

"All right," Haley agreed.

Sarah was full of energy. Off we went to see the lions and then the giraffes. The giraffes were one of my favorite animals.

It was a beautiful day so we spent most of our time at outside exhibits. But we did stop in to see the new baby gorillas. They were in a small building which only had enough room for a few visitors at a time.

The mother and two baby gorillas were resting. We watched them for quite a long time.

"The mother is big!" Haley said.

"I think she's looking at you," I told Haley, nudging her in the arm.

Seemingly unaffected by our stares, the gorilla

stretched her big arms wide and yawned. She was probably used to having people watch her.

After a while, she climbed up a tree and sat quietly gazing at us. Then without any warning at all, she jumped down, and landed right in front of us.

Startled by her sudden movement, everyone gasped and moved back a bit. My eyes opened wide but I wasn't scared. Although, I was relieved that there was a thick piece of safety glass between us and the gorilla.

A little boy standing near us started to cry.

"Don't worry. The glass is very strong. It won't break," I told the little boy, hoping that would lessen his fears.

His mother confirmed what I had said, telling him there was absolutely nothing to worry about.

The mother gorilla continued to look us right in the eye. "She is just protecting her babies," my father said. But that didn't convince Sarah who had rushed to Mother's side.

"I'm hungry. Let's go," Sarah begged, wanting to leave more from fear than hunger.

So the little boy wouldn't hear me, I whispered in Haley's ear, "The gorilla really does look like she could break right through the glass!"

"Don't even think it, Kathryn," said Haley, grabbing my arm and squeezing it.

"I'm only kidding," I said as we turned and left

17

Was It Different?

Once outside, we began pleading and begging, "Can we eat now, Mom? Can we?" Most of the time, we brought our own picnic lunches to the zoo but today was different.

"Okay, if you girls are that hungry, we can eat now," Mother replied.

"Hurrah!" Sarah cheered.

I saw my father's eyes light up at the mention of food. "Yes, let's eat," he said.

At the crowded restaurant we got in line. The smell of the food made my mouth water. I could almost taste the french fries. The line was pretty long so our parents suggested that the three of us go and save a table before they were all taken.

"Good idea," Haley said.

"Okay," I agreed.

"We'll be there in a few minutes with the food," Mother said to us as we left the line.

Sarah raced ahead and found a table. We tried to follow her but did not get far because there were chairs and tables in the way. As we slowly made our way through the maze of chairs and tables, a cute little girl with big blue eyes and long black curly hair stood right in front of us. She looked lost. Standing there clutching a tattered, faded blanket, I thought she was going to start crying at any moment.

"Hi," I said softly. She didn't answer or move but instead, pulled her blanket up closer to her face, and held on to it even tighter.

"Excuse us," Haley said, starting to wheel toward her. Still the little girl didn't move.

"Please, could you move over a little so that we could get by," I asked her quietly again.

Still she didn't budge. Her eyes opened even wider and started to fill with tears. "Oh, no," I whispered. "She's going to cry."

"Her mother is probably in line getting their food," I told Haley.

"Kathryn, why don't you ask her to move again," Haley suggested.

"Where's your mother?" I asked her instead. The little girl kept right on standing there, not saying a word. Then her lips started to quiver and she burst into tears.

"Everything's all right. Don't cry," I said. "Is your mother getting you something to eat?"

No response and she started crying all over again.

"Why does she keep staring at us and crying?" Haley asked confused by the little girl's reaction.

"She's probably afraid because her mother isn't with her," I told Haley.

Haley looked at me, then at the little girl, and then back at me. "Afraid of what?" she asked.

"Frightened of strangers, silly!" I cried.

82

"Oh," said Haley.

"Please move over so that we can get by," Haley pleaded. The little girl was between us and the table that Sarah was saving for us.

Suddenly, the little girl started to cry even louder, "Waaaaah, Waaaaah." She kept wailing. We looked at each other baffled. Why? Now what?

It seemed like everyone in the restaurant was looking at us now. "Maybe she's lost?" Haley suggested. "Or her mother's in line getting food?"

"Are you lost little girl?" Sarah asked her softly. Sarah was standing by our table and behind the little girl. Sarah bent down to talk to her but that must have scared her because she cried even louder.

"Waaaah!" she cried.

"You're all right," I told the little girl, trying to comfort her.

Minutes were starting to seem more like hours. "Are you upset because you want your mother?" Sarah asked while glancing around the room, hoping that she would appear.

"I wish she would stop crying," said Haley.

We had no choice but to wait since she wouldn't move and she wouldn't stop bawling. "Let's back up so people can get by us. Okay?" I suggested.

Haley agreed. Just as we started to wheel backwards, the little girl's mother arrived with their food.

"What's the matter, Emily?" she asked her.

"Waaaah," was Emily's response as her tiny hands pointed in our direction. The mother was trying to calm her daughter, but Emily still refused to be comforted.

"Would you like some help carrying the food to your table?" Sarah asked politely.

"No, but thanks anyway," said Emily's mother.

Best Friends

"Great idea to offer to help, Sarah," I thought while sitting there feeling rather helpless.

"It's all right, don't cry Emily. These girls won't hurt you. They're just handicapped," her mother said, as she reached down to take her daughter's hand. Emily was pulling and tugging on her mother's arm as they walked toward their table.

"Sorry, girls," the woman said as she turned and gave us a sympathetic look over her shoulder.

"It's okay," I replied, continuing to watch them. Emily was still whimpering and her mother was still trying to console and calm her.

Once they were gone, it was like a dark cloud had moved away. "Wow! That was horrible, " I thought.

We were very happy her mother had returned and saved tearful little Emily. We looked at each other, shook our heads, smiled and wheeled to our table. We were famished and could only think about food at the moment.

"Phew! I'm glad that's over," whispered Haley. "I'm hungry."

As if on cue, my parents appeared on the scene with their trays piled high with food.

"Hurrah," I said, hungry and relieved to think about something else. We ate quickly and were ready to move on in no time.

After eating, we were ready for more action. "Let's go to the petting zoo and then to the aquarium," Sarah suggested.

"Sounds good to me," Haley replied.

"We'd better hurry. Soon my parents will get tired and will want to go home, " I whispered to Haley.

"Okay. Let's get going then," she replied.

We were off to the petting zoo which was the closest exhibit to the restaurant. At the petting zoo, we wheeled right in with all of the animals. The animals sniffed and licked us.

"They really like the wheelchairs!" said Haley who was carefully watching a baby goat.

The next thing we knew, the baby goat ran under Haley's wheelchair, lay down and wouldn't budge. He must have enjoyed the shade on such a sunny day.

"They like to sniff the wheels. I think they're curious because they haven't seen many wheelchairs," I said.

"Probably not," Haley replied.

"We're going to the aquarium, are you coming?" Sarah asked.

"Okay," said Haley.

"Sarah, watch the little goats so they don't run out when we start to wheel away," I told Sarah.

"Sure," Sarah replied.

Once the goats were safe, we were ready to see the fish. As we wheeled to the aquarium, Haley became very serious. "Wasn't it embarrassing?" she asked.

"What?" I asked even though I knew what she was going to say.

"You know. That little girl. Emily. The one who wouldn't stop crying or move over and let us wheel by her?"

"Yes, it was embarrassing," I replied, realizing Haley was still very upset about what had happened at the restaurant.

"I think Emily was afraid of us because we were in the wheelchairs!" Haley stated firmly.

"Maybe, but she might have been afraid because her mother wasn't with her," I suggested.

"I don't think so! Besides, afraid or not, her mother didn't have to call us 'handicapped'!" Haley replied.

Surprised by Haley's reaction, I told her, "I don't think she meant to hurt your feelings."

"Well, she did! And she meant to!" Haley protested.

I was at a loss for words.

Scowling, Haley continued, "Kathryn, don't your feelings get hurt when people act like they are afraid of you? Or when they call you 'handicapped'?" Haley asked.

I thought about what she had said for a moment. I stopped and turned to answer her, "Sure, I feel badly. But most of the time, it is only because people just don't understand."

Still looking pretty upset, Haley said, "But that little girl's mother didn't even try to understand. She wanted to be mean."

Trying to convince her otherwise, I explained, "Sometimes people use words they don't think are hurtful."

"But she said I was handicapped and I'm not!" Haley said.

"But I'm handicapped," I said, looking her right in the eyes.

"Well, I don't care. I'm not and the lady meant it to be mean," Haley replied.

"Haley you're not afraid of differences. You don't seem to notice them. If you do, you don't treat people differently because of them. Do you?" I asked.

"Maybe! And maybe not," she replied stubbornly, turning her head away.

"Not everyone is like you. I wish they were," I told her.

Suddenly, we heard my mother calling, "Hurry you two! We'll never get there if you don't move faster."

"Coming!" I yelled back to her.

Haley seemed calmer and less agitated as she spoke, "Thanks for listening, Kathryn. What you said makes sense. And I'm glad I'm not like that lady! Coming from you, it means a lot to me."

Well, at least she was starting to feel better. I could hear it in her voice.

My mother was waiting for us as we made our way toward the aquarium building,

"What took you two so long?" Mother asked when we reached her.

"Oh, nothing," I told her. It was our secret.

Only one hill left to go. "Haley, I'll race you the rest of the way to the aquarium!" I challenged her.

"Go!" she yelled, daring me to beat her. We started wheeling up the hill.

"Come on," I said, "You can go faster than that!"

She laughed and really leaned forward to get more speed. Haley was breathing heavy and working hard to wheel up the hill.

Haley shouted, "I'm trying to get there. Wait for me, please!"

"Let's go, Haley. You too, Mom," I called as I began to race ahead.

It was slow going up the steep incline. I knew once we made it to the top it would be much easier to wheel. We could go much faster. Watching Haley speed pass me, I thought--she was almost ready for wheelies.

I wheeled with all my might, trying to catch her. But we made it to the aquarium doors at the same time.

"Tie!" I screamed, knowing it was very close.

"Tied again?" she asked, sounding discouraged. "I thought for sure I'd beaten you this time."

"Well, it was pretty close," I admitted.

My mother held the big doors open while we rushed through them. She seemed tired; I knew the signs.

"Hurry, Haley! My mom looks tired and that

means we'll be leaving soon," I whispered.

In the aquarium we saw some amazing sights and had a spectacular time. But it wasn't long before my parents were too exhausted to go on.

They were sitting and talking by the exit area of the aquarium, waiting patiently for us.

After a while we heard them calling, "Hurry girls. It's getting late."

"We're coming," I assured them. We meandered toward the exit, taking our time and stopping along the way to see a few more fish.

Another fun filled day at the zoo had come to an end.

On the drive home, I couldn't resist asking Haley, "Well, was it different?"

Confused, she asked, " What?" But from the smile on her face, I knew she remembered.

I asked again, "Was it different going to the zoo using the wheelchair instead of walking?"

"Yes! It really was different," Haley answered. She talked about why it seemed different to her which made me laugh.

Sarah had been listening intently. "It really is different, huh, Haley?" Sarah asked her.

Haley, with a grin on her face, just nodded in agreement.

"Well, it wasn't different for me," I told them.

First they looked at each other and then back at me. They saw the humor in what I had said and we burst into laughter.

We were sure exhausted after spending the day wheeling around at the zoo. And the three of us dozed off on the way home.

18

Ready for Wheelies!

The next week was more of the same for Haley. She was becoming an expert in using the wheelchair. Haley's strength and her endurance had really increased. She was very confident. Moving around the classroom in her wheelchair became easier every day. It was still crowded but no one seemed to mind.

I looked forward to recess more than ever before. It was wonderful to share things with my best friend. We had never explored as much as we did these past two weeks. Recess had become quite an adventure. I felt like I was living in a world like Linda's.

The weather was still unseasonably warm. In the classroom there was hardly a breeze. Everyone was anxious for recess just to cool off. When the bell finally did ring, screams of joy could be heard throughout the school. Even some teachers voices were recognizable among the screams. It was that hot!

Everyone rushed for the door faster than I had ever seen them. By the time Haley and I reached the doorway, the room had emptied.

I looked at Haley as we wheeled out together. With my best friend in a wheelchair wheeling around with me, recess was altogether different.

"I love recess," yelled Haley.

We spotted everyone over by the basketball hoops. I turned to Haley, asking, "Let's race to get to them. All right?"

She agreed.

"Let the race begin!" bellowed Haley with a roar. We wheeled as fast as we could.

"Can't catch me," she screamed as loud as she could. Haley took the lead.

She was strong! I tried but I couldn't push any harder. Whewwwww! It took a lot of effort to try to catch up with her! I pushed with all of my strength using every muscle in my body.

"You're fast, Haley!" I shouted to her.

Then I really concentrated on putting every ounce of power that I could muster into wheeling. I had caught up to her and we were neck and neck.

We looked each other right in the eye for a split second. "Remember Miss Martin's rules for wheelchair safety'," I reminded her, trying to get her to laugh.

"I remember," she replied.

Then she began putting on the pressure. She slowly moved ahead until she was in front of me again. I was losing speed. Had she been practicing? I knew that it would be difficult to catch up to her now. I was too slow.

All of our friends stood together at the edge of the basketball court waving and cheering.

"I won," she shouted, throwing her arms in the air. She turned and watched me wheel the final couple of feet.

"What a race!" Jessica shouted.

"Big change from the first day we raced, huh?" Haley replied.

"You're ready for wheelies now!" I shouted, still trying to catch my breath.

"Ready for wheelies!" Linda yelled, joining in the cheer. "Ready for wheelies!"

"Thanks," replied Haley, blushing.

Then Cassie turned to me and asked, "Kathryn, exactly what are wheelies?"

"What? You don't know what wheelies are? You're joking, right?" Linda said, chiding her.

Cassie turned beet red.

"Linda!" Jessica said, "Stop it!"

"Oh, everyone is too sensitive," Linda replied.

"Cassie, it's nothing really. It's just a saying. It means 'you are good at wheeling, or racing or doing fancy turns'," I explained, quoting another friend who used a wheelchair.

"Oh," Cassie said.

"I knew that," insisted Haley.

"I can tell your leg doesn't hurt as much," said Linda.

"I guess the race proved it," said Haley, nodding her head. She raised her leg a little and wiggled her toes on the broken leg. "You're right, Linda!"

Haley and Linda had everyone laughing.

"Let's go sit on the benches by the oak tree and chat until the end of recess," suggested Kelsey.

"Great idea," said Cassie who loved Linda's stories.

"A good tale of adventure," was Jessica's request.

Haley had everyone howling with her version of our trip to the zoo. We shared some other funny tales that happened that day.

Linda leaned over and whispered in my ear, "I'd like to try going to the zoo in your wheelchair too."

Without looking at her, I knew Linda was serious. "Lindaaa!" I said, laughing so hard that I was crying.

Linda had this sheepish grin on her face. I knew she was daydreaming about an adventure at the zoo in my wheelchair. Unfortunately, at that moment, the bell rang!

19

Between Friends

Late summer passed into early fall. It was such a beautiful and peaceful time of year. The trees were full but starting to get a tinge of color, the first sign that the leaves would soon be dropping.

We spent many hours sitting, talking and enjoying our friendship on Haley's front porch. It was our special place. The view of the trees, the yard and the neighborhood made it such a comfortable place to study.

One afternnoon, while we were doing our homework on the porch, enjoying each others company, I told Haley (for the millionth time!), "This really is a great place to study, Haley."

"Thanks, Kathryn," Haley replied, proud of the special place.

"I seem to get more homework done whenever we sit out here," I told her.

Haley nodded in agreement.

Sitting there in the splendid quiet, I thought about how Haley's time in the wheelchair was coming to an end. The days were going by faster than I wanted but I knew they were going too slow for Haley.

The first week was difficult for her because she had to adjust to life without walking. During her time in the wheelchair, Haley had learned so much about not being able to walk. A smile came to my face just thinking about her first day.

I stared at Haley, carefully observing her and wondering why she seemed so different to me now? Probably because she understood my world so much better after being in a wheelchair. My parents didn't always understand but now at least my best friend did.

While it lasted, it was wonderful to have someone to really be with at school. Wheeling with my best friend to recess, to lunch, to gym, to class was incredible. We went places and did things that I had never tried before.

Haley also seemed to enjoy the time we spent together. I found myself wanting her leg to heal. Yet, at the same time, I was wishing she could wheel around with me forever.

Knowing her time in the wheelchair was almost over, Haley explained she was thinking about a lot of things which had to do with being in the wheelchair. Things that we'd never really talked about before.

Haley asked me, "Is it lonely being the only one at school using a wheelchair?"

I wasn't surprised by her question, people had asked it before. But after the last few weeks of being with her in the wheelchair, it was a much more difficult question to answer.

Getting a little choked up, I breathed in deeply and then I tried to explain, "Some days, I feel more alone than others but everyone feels alone at times."

"Oh," she said in a hushed voice.

"Haley, when you're walking again, I will really miss having you to wheel around with," I told her.

Haley was quiet and thoughtful. "I wish you could walk and run!" she said. "Don't you?"

Watching her worried eyes filled with concern, I thought, would she understand? Could she? Could anyone who walked ever really understand?

I tried to explain, "I don't really think about it often. I use the wheelchair because I can't walk."

Haley still looked bewildered and confused.

If anyone who walked could understand how I felt, I knew in my heart that Haley would.

I coughed to clear my throat. I watched her for a minute. She was my best friend. On the spur of the moment, I began to talk more openly about my feelings than I had ever done before in my life.

"Some days are harder than others. When I can't wheel off of a curb or into a building, I get angry. Then I wish I could walk. When people act like I'm invisible, then I wish I could walk. When people treat me differently because they don't understand, then I wish I could walk," I said, looking straight into her eyes.

I wanted her to know how it was in my world. I wanted her friendship but not her pity. Her eyes began to fill with water. Had I said too much?

Haley's chin dropped to her chest and putting her hands to her face, she quietly started to cry. I was filled with emotion observing her reaction. I knew that she needed some time to compose herself. I waited.

"I wish you could walk too," Haley said. Her voice was barely audible.

I reached over, touched her hand and tried to explain, "I'm not unhappy because I use a wheelchair."

Haley said apologetically, "Oh, I didn't mean to

say that you were, Kathryn."

"I know," I answered softly.

Still trying to help her to understand, I told her, "Haley, I enjoy watching people run, jump, climb, dance and do exciting or athletic things. It's wonderful. I don't look at them and feel sad. I just want to join them. To do whatever I can do. To try." She listened attentively.

"I may do it differently but I am running, I am jumping, and I am dancing. How I do it may not look the same but it feels the same," I said, adding, *"Being included is what counts!"*

Haley smiled and seemed more relaxed. She understood what I meant because all of our friends wanted to be included.

"That's why I enjoy Linda so much. She does things differently too," I said. "Linda does things that I can't do. That's why we all love to hear her outrageous tales of adventure."

"Yeah," Haley agreed, nodding her head. "Now that I think about it, you're right. You're always trying to get me to do wild and daring things," she replied with her hands on her hips.

"No way! Not me! You're the wild one!" I replied.

"You're pretty fearless, Kathryn. You try everything without complaining and you can't even walk," Haley said.

"You make me sound awfully good," I told her, embarrassed by the compliments.

We went back to doing our school work. My eyes focused on my book. I continued reading where I'd left off, but my thoughts weren't on the printed words. My mind kept drifting as I thought about how much we were alike. Haley believed, like I did, that being your best meant trying your best. Memories of the past few weeks brought another smile to my face.

We kept trying to finish our homework. Haley kept asking me to pass one book or another. She seemed distracted. I could tell she still had something on her mind too.

In the middle of reading about colonial life, Haley asked me another one of her serious questions. "Life in a wheelchair really is different, isn't it?"

"Yeah, it's different all right, different from life with walking legs," I replied. "Like you, you're different!"

"What?" she cried.

Haley had thrown her notebook at me but I ducked as the book flew by. "Missed me," I yelled.

"Yeah, you're my best friend with the walking legs," I told her. "I'll treat you the same even though your different!"

"How am I different?" Haley protested. "Kathryn look again," she said with a twinkle in her eye. "I don't have 'walking legs' until my cast comes off!"

I smiled watching her lift her leg with the cast high in the air. We settled down again and went back to our studies.

Suddenly, Haley looked up from her book. "Kathryn, we're not like that mean lady at the zoo," she said. "She only saw our differences, not us."

"Uh-huh," I replied. I had forgotten about the lady at the zoo. She had really upset Haley that day. No one had ever treated Haley like that before. "She just didn't understand," I reminded her.

"Yes she did," Haley insisted. "If she wasn't mean, then why did she call us 'handicapped'?"

"Haley, the word 'handicapped' isn't a bad word. It's only a word. How people treat you is more important," I said.

"I guess so, Kathryn," Haley replied, still uncertain about whether she agreed.

96

The peacefulness of the porch lulled us back into our silent reading. We sat there for what seemed like hours, finishing our assignments. The afternoon had disappeared and it would be dark shortly. It was quite an afternoon, one I would remember for a long time.

As we were finishing up, we heard my dad honking the horn as he pulled up in front of her house. As I gathered up my books to leave, Haley leaned closer to me and whispered, "I really do understand, Kathryn. But I still wish that you could walk."

We said goodbye. It was time for me to go home.

20

Walking Again!

It was late at night and I was ready to go to bed when the telephone rang. "Kathryn, it's for you," Mother called from the kitchen.

"Okay, I'm coming," I yelled as I wheeled into the kitchen.

Mother handed me the telephone. "It's Haley. She has good news for you," she said, smiling.

"Hi, Haley," I said talking into the telephone. I was very surprised by the late night phone call.

"I can walk," Haley screamed. "I can walk again!"

"Wow! That's great!" I replied.

She went on to explain she had been to the doctor that afternoon. "The doctor took off my big cast and put on a walking cast."

"What's a walking cast?" I asked.

"It's a softer and much smaller cast. I can walk on it but I still can't run or jump. And, tomorrow's the big day, Kathryn," she said. "My first day back to school with my new walking cast."

"I can't wait to see what the new cast looks like!" I said, hearing the excitement in her voice.

Walking Again!

"No more wheelchair!" Haley screamed. She was so thrilled I couldn't stop myself from smiling.

"I'm happy for you!" I told her.

Then I heard her mother in the background, "Haley, get to bed, right now!" she yelled. "Or you'll be too tired to go to school tomorrow."

"My mom's calling me. I have to go," Haley apologized. "I'll see you tomorrow."

"Okay," I replied.

"At the bus stop!" she screamed into the phone before she hung up.

"Bye," I called to her, knowing she didn't hear me because the telephone had already disconnected and the dial tone was ringing in my ear.

"Wow! Haley, walking again!" I said aloud as I went from the kitchen straight to my room and to bed.

Before going to sleep, I lay in bed thinking about Haley walking again. Tomorrow would be her first day without the wheelchair. I was having mixed feelings. My heart was heavy when I thought about wheeling around school alone. No more Haley wheeling beside me, looking for trouble, for action, for fun! Yet, I was happy for Haley.

Before I knew it, I had drifted off to sleep. I awoke to my alarm clock screaming at me to get up. I quickly got ready for school, making sure I didn't miss the bus.

When the bus pulled up to the school, Haley was waiting for me just like I had waited for her.

"Hi, Haley," I yelled out the bus window.

"Wow, you're walking again!" screamed Sarah.

Sarah seemed so surprised. Had I forgotten to tell her?

"Hi, Sarah! Hi, Kathryn!" Haley replied.

"It's great that you can walk again," I said as I was getting off of the bus.

Sarah was off and gone in a flash. She was quick.

"Well, how does it feel to be walking again?" I asked her.

"It feels really good. But I'll be happier when I don't need this dumb walking cast either," she complained.

"Be patient," I reminded her. "You're right about the walking cast being smaller."

We went into the classroom. Everyone started circling Haley. They asked her a million questions: "Where's the wheelchair? How does it feel to walk again? Why do you still have a cast on your leg? Did you save the other cast with all of our autographs?" Haley tried to answer all of their questions but was starting to get flustered.

The teacher came over to see the special new cast. Everyone was busy signing it. "Good to see you walking again, Haley," Mrs. McConnell said in her gentle voice. She could make anyone feel good. Then she reached down to add her signature to the new cast with her bright red marking pen.

Haley was still answering questions. "I still can't run or jump. My doctor made me this special walking cast so I could get out the wheelchair and start walking again," she explained.

"Well, it must feel good to be up and about," said Mrs. McConnell.

"And to be out of the wheelchair!" interrupted Linda.

Watching Haley walk with the new cast, I realized how fast her time in the wheelchair had gone. It seemed like only yesterday she first came back to school in the wheelchair. Where had the days gone?

Already on the other side of the classroom, Haley was busy playing with Henry the hamster. She could get a closer look at him now that she was up on her feet again.

Walking Again!

"It sure feels good to be able to take the hamster out of the cage by myself," I heard Haley say to Jessica.

Cassie, who was standing near them, asked, "You must be happy about being able to walk again."

Linda slapped Haley on the back and said, "Glad to be walking, I'll bet."

"Yeah, it feels great!" Haley said still grimacing over the slap on the back.

"I hope I never break my leg. Especially, compound fractures!" Linda told her.

Wanting to join their lively discussion, I yelled across the room to Haley, "The hamster is glad you're walking again!"

"Thanks," she said busy stroking the fur of our class pet. "Kathryn, do you want to hold the hamster?" she asked, bringing Henry over to me.

"Sure," I replied. In the blink of an eye, she was already at my side, and putting him on my lap.

"Thanks," I said, starting to rub the back of the little, furry creature.

Henry's claws were digging into my leg. "Watch out, he might have an accident on you, Kathryn," Linda said jokingly which made us chuckle.

"I'd better put Henry back in his cage," Haley said. "Remember what happened to me?"

"How could I forget!" I replied.

"That little episode is imprinted forever in my memory," Linda shouted.

Haley helped me to carefully remove his little claws from my shorts before she picked him up. "Thanks for bringing him over for me to hold," I told her.

Then I wheeled behind Haley, following her to Henry's cage and watched her carefully put him back in his cage. We tried to get him to eat but he wasn't interested.

"Kathryn, guess what the nicest part about being out of the wheelchair is?" she asked me.

"I don't know. What?" I replied.

"Being able to get my brother back when he bothers me. Now I can chase him all over the house!" she answered. Haley and I started to laugh.

Jessica leaned over and said, "Shhhhhh! Class is starting. You're going to get into trouble."

"Thanks, Jessica," I responded.

We rushed back to our desks to avoid losing recess. The day seemed to go by in slow motion.

Sitting in class, I couldn't stop myself from daydreaming and thinking about the last few weeks. Wondering. Would everything be the same as before? Could it ever be the same again?

I was staring out the window when I heard, "Pssst, Kathryn," Haley whispered. "Pay attention. Don't you hear the teacher? Kathryn!"

"What?" I said, unaware of what was happening and realizing Haley was talking to me.

"Kathryn, haven't you heard Mrs. McConnell? She has already called your name twice. Pay attention or you're going to lose recess!" she warned me with a real look of concern on her face.

"But I wasn't talking," I said.

I tried desperately to look busy and find my place. Had I read this page already? I couldn't remember. Where was I? What section of the book was the class looking at? I needed to find my page before I got into trouble.

"Kathryn!" Mrs. McConnell called my name again.

"Yes," I answered her, still busy looking for the right place in the book.

"Kathryn!" Mrs. McConnell repeated in a stern voice. "Pay attention!"

"I didn't hear you," I said apologetically.

Feeling more fragile today, I wasn't my usual confident self.

Time drifted by and soon it was recess but I didn't rush out. I lingered, taking my time, even pretending to look for something. I wanted to be alone.

But Haley stayed by my side and didn't leave when the bell rang.

"Haley, don't feel like you have to wait for me. Go ahead. I can catch up with you. Don't wait!" I told her.

"Oh, and why not?" she asked bewildered. "Kathryn, I always wait for you."

Avoiding her eyes, I said, "I just don't want you to feel like you have to wait for me."

Haley didn't move. Instead, she sat down next to me and asked, "Kathryn? Don't you want me to wait?"

I was embarrassed because I had been feeling sorry for myself, daydreaming, and pouting all morning. "Yes, I want you to wait for me," I admitted to her.

"Well, let's go then!" Haley said already up and moving toward the door.

I unlocked my wheelchair and pushed. As we left the room, I thought about what she had said and she was right; she had always waited for me.

"Come on. Let's race. You in the wheelchair against me in the walking cast!" she yelled.

"You're not supposed to run in that cast!" I reminded her.

"Okay!" she replied. "You sound just like my mother!"

As she walked and I wheeled toward the tetherball court, my eyes started to fill with tears. I fought back the flood of tears the best that I could. Why was I crying, anyway? I wiped my eyes dry as quickly as I could with my arm, not wanting Haley or anyone else

103

to see them.

When I was sure that any proof of my tears had vanished, I said, "You'll be out of the 'walking cast' before you know it." I knew she needed cheering up as well as me.

"I know, " Haley replied, "I can hardly wait."

The next moment, we were startled by familiar screams, and we both glanced up. The sounds were coming from across the playground. Haley and I looked at each other. We couldn't believe it--no, on second thought, we could believe it. It was Linda!

"Hey! You two slow pokes! Run! I mean walk! I mean wheel!" she shouted. Linda was one friend who could make us laugh anywhere, anytime; she never changed.

"Linda, we're coming," I shouted as we did just what she had asked. I wheeled and Haley walked over to where she was. We laughed over Linda's boisterous and wild behavior.

"I'm glad you're laughing and smiling again," Haley said. "The Kathryn I know is back!"

"Thanks," I replied. "I didn't know I had gone anywhere."

"You've been quiet all morning," she told me.

"I have?" I said, knowing in my heart that it was true.

"I guess I'd be sad if I had to keep using the wheelchair," Haley said.

"We'll always be able to run and wheel together!" I told her.

"What? Of course we'll be able to run and wheel together," she responded.

"I thought things would be different with you walking again," I admitted to her. "I thought our friendship was going to change."

She listened until I had finished. "Things haven't

changed, Kathryn," Haley said. "We're still best friends."

"I know that now, " I told her.

When we got to the tetherball court we got in line after Linda. She was talking a mile a minute. Haley and I listened to Linda and waited for our turn.

"You're up next!" Jessica yelled.

"Your serve, Haley," I told her.

"All right!" she replied taking the ball and getting ready to hit it. "Remember to duck!" Haley screamed as she clobbered the ball.

"Listen to her, reminding me how to avoid getting hit by the ball," I thought to myself.

"You're funny, Haley," I told her as I returned her serve.

"Not me, Kathryn. You're the funny one," she yelled. Then she really slammed it again. "Kaaaa booom!" It was moving through the air pretty fast.

"Wow!" I said. "You're good!"

Haley smacked the ball again and again. My arm was getting tired.

"Duck," Haley yelled.

I did.

She was awfully good. Winning wasn't going to be easy. We continued to play, volleying the ball back and forth around the pole. It was the longest game we'd ever played. We didn't want it to end but it had.

"Yes!" I screamed. "I won!"

"How did you beat me?" Haley said.

"I don't know! I just hit the ball and I ducked," I said with a gleam in my eye.

"Oh, sure," Haley said.

"It's all right. You'll have other chances to beat me," I told her. " But you'd better practice."

We laughed until we could laugh no more.

Haley volunteered to push my wheelchair back to

class.

"I'm not that tired," I told her.

"You should be tired after the game we just played!" she insisted.

"Okay, since I won the game, you can push me," I agreed.

As Haley pushed me back to class, my body relaxed and I realized she was right, I was tired.

I thought about how everything was different now that she had come back to school walking. But what a day we'd had. My world had not changed like I thought it would. Things weren't the same but they were still pretty good.

"Thanks for helping me, Haley," I told her. "I am more tired than I thought. I have to play hard to beat you. You're so good!"

"Next time, I'll beat you!" Haley promised.

"Don't be so sure," I said. She poked me in the shoulder, and we laughed.

As she held the classroom door open for me, I said, "Thanks, Haley."

"You're welcome," she replied.

Haley had a funny smirk on her face. Why was she looking at me like that? "Haley, what are you smiling about?" I asked.

"Oh, it's nothing Kathryn," she replied. "You'll remember later."

Going into the classroom, I tried to think what she could possibly mean by "I'll remember later". Remember what?

21

"It's not your Birthday?"

The rest of the day went by as quickly as recess. On the bus ride home, I didn't want to talk. Instead, I sat quietly contemplating all that had happened. It had been my first day without my best friend wheeling around school with me.

Part of me knew I would miss Haley using a wheelchair but I was happy for her. I would see Haley first, not her walking legs; just as she always sees me first, not my wheelchair. We were closer friends now than ever before. How lucky could a person be, I thought.

Sarah's tugging on my shirt and the sound of the squeaky brakes as the bus came to a complete stop, let me know that we were home at last. In seconds, we exited the bus and were rushing into the house.

"Mother!" Sarah shouted as we entered the kitchen.

"Get a snack and I'll be right in," she yelled from another part of the house.

"Okay," I responded, following closely behind Sarah.

"What is this?" Sarah cried out, standing at the

table with her back to me. As I wheeled up to the table to see what it was, I was just as surprised as Sarah by what I saw.

"Who's the package for, Mom?" I shouted to her.

"Read the tag that's on the box," she called to us.

Sarah lifted the tag and read it, "To Kathryn"

Hundreds of goose bumps popped up all over my body. "A present for me," I said.

Sarah couldn't believe it either. "Well, it's got your name on it," she said. "It must be yours."

Her eyes were wide open just like mine. We stared at the package.

"It's not your birthday," Sarah insisted. "Why did you get a present?".

"I don't know," I admitted, wondering the same thing.

The package was beautiful. It had shiny red paper with an incredible yellow and red shiny ribbon. I hated to rip it open, but sacrifices had to be made.

The outside wrapping fell away once the ribbon was untied. Inside, there was another wrapped package.

"There's another one," Sarah yelled.

"And a note too!" I said, hesitating.

Sarah pursed her lips and replied, "Come on Kathryn, open the present and read the note later."

"All right!" I replied.

The smaller box was wrapped with even more beautiful paper and ribbon than the first.

I unwrapped the second box with help from Sarah who picked up the ribbons as they fell from the package. Sarah mumbled something but I wasn't listening.

"Wow! It's the computer program that I wanted!" I shouted with sheer delight. I had been saving my allowance for weeks to buy it. But who could have known?

108

Mother entered the kitchen and asked, "Well, who's it from, Kathryn?"

"I haven't opened the note," I responded.

"Well, open it and find out," she suggested.

I reached down, picked up the note from the table, tore open the envelope, slid out the card and read it silently. A smile slowly appeared on my face as my mouth curved into the biggest grin. At that moment, I remembered something Haley had said to me at school.

Impatient and eager to know who it was from, Sarah insisted, "Come on, Kathryn. Read it aloud!"

"Okay!" I replied, getting a little choked up. Sitting back in my wheelchair with my shoulders resting comfortably, I readjusted my eyeglasses, cleared my throat, and read the note aloud:

Dear Kathryn,
Thank you for sharing your wheelchair with me. You helped me to do things on my own.
    Love,
Your best friend with the walking legs.

Overwhelmed both by Haley's understanding and our friendship, I was unable to stop the flood of tears I had been holding back all day.

My mother leaned over, hugged me really tight, and whispered in my ear, "Kathryn, we love you! And we are very proud of you."

I hugged her back as tightly as I could. I gazed into her loving face and knew it didn't really matter if they did use the "I" word again because I knew I was *independent*.

Hope Benton, Author

Hope Benton is the pen name used by the author Beatrice Hope Benton-Borghi. She has travelled and lived all over the world.

Hope is an experienced teacher and grant writer who earned her B.A. in Chemistry from North Adams State College in Massachusetts, and her M.Ed. from Boston University, Boston, Massachusetts.

She taught Chemistry at the high school level for over a decade in both public and private schools in the United States and Munich, West Germany.

Hope has been honored by inclusion in the following books: Who's Who of American Women, Who's Who in Education, Who's Who in the Midwest, and Who's Who of Emerging Leaders.

The author, whose child and brother both have physical challenges, has written stories with an emphasis on the similarities among children. The social interactions, unique relationships and adventures of the characters are based on "real life " stories.

Lynne Srba, Illustrator

Lynne Srba is an artist living in Raleigh, North Carolina. Lynne has travelled extensively in the U.S. and Europe.

Lynne studied at the Columbus College of Art and Design in Ohio, and the North Carolina State University School of Design, from which she earned her master's degree.

She has worked with universities, colleges, museums, publishers, agencies, individuals, and corporations, producing original works of art. Lynne has won regional and national awards for illustration, design, and fine art.

Lynne paints and draws angels and the landscapes and seascapes that they inhabit. Her angels are the children, friends, family, and animals that we love.

Her work can be seen in galleries, museums, books, private and corporate collections in the United States, Europe. and at her studio in Raleigh, North Carolina